PIERRE AND MARIE

Adapted by
Ron Clark

Based on the play
Les Palmes de M. Schutz
by
Jean-Noël Fenwick

SAMUEL FRENCH, INC.

45 West 25th Street
NEW YORK 10010
LONDON

7623 Sunset Boulevard
HOLLYWOOD 90046
TORONTO

ISBN 0 573 62919 6   Printed in U.S.A.   #17841

IMPORTANT BILLING AND CREDIT REQUIREMENTS

All producers of PIERRE AND MARIE *must* give credit to the Authors of the Play in all programs distributed in connection with performances of the Play and in all instances in which the title of the Play appears for purposes of advertising, publicizing or otherwise exploiting the Play and/or a production. The names *must* appear on a separate lines, on which no other name appears, immediately following the title, and *must* appear in size of type as stipulated below:

(NAME OF PRODUCER)
presents

PIERRE AND MARIE   *(100%)*

Adapted by
Ron Clark   *(not less than 50%)*

Based on the play, *Les Palmes de M. Schutz* by
Jean-Nöel Fenwick   *(not less than 25%)*

ACT 1

Scene 1

AT RISE: We are in a science laboratory in the late 1800's, in Paris. Stage left has several wooden tables on which sit a number of scientific apparati. Bunsen burners, beakers, test tubes, etc., etc. Stage right, has a coal-burning stove with a pipe that leads up into the ceiling, a smaller table, not far from the stove, a blackboard with chalk and an eraser, and a pencil sharpener. There is also an armoire against one of the walls and a desk.

The large room faces a street. It is actually below street level, so that when entering the lab one has to step down several stairs.

Through the window we can see that it is snowing lightly. There is very little light in the laboratory. The pendulum clock on the wall indicates that it's 7:30 A.M., and whatever light there is at present is that of any early winter morning.

(The front door opens and PIERRE CURIE, thirtyish, enters. He is sporting a beard and his hair is worn in a sort of brush cut. He is all bundled up in a black, worn-out overcoat. He is obviously freezing. He is carrying a briefcase, which looks more like a student's bookbag, half torn. He puts it on the central table, then goes about shivering as he tries to warm up, smacking his arms across his body.

PIERRE is wearing mittens. He goes to the stove, opens it, looks into it, and then looks at the empty coal bin.)

PIERRE. *(All the while shivering.)* Still no coal.

(He goes to the coat rack, which is holding two white smocks. He is trying to decide whether or not to change into a smock. He removes his coat, all the while making shivering noises. He realizes

that his mittens are attached to his coat, much the way a mother would attach her four-year-old's mittens.

PIERRE *starts hanging up his overcoat while grabbing the smock, and in so doing, he's getting everything mixed up. He finally gets the smock on. He's colder than ever. He flings off one of his smock sleeves and quickly gets his overcoat and puts it back on. He rubs his hands together and taps his feet.*

He suddenly notices part of his smock hanging on the back of his coat. He tries reaching for it but can't. He gives up and goes to the table on which he deposited his briefcase.

PIERRE *opens his briefcase/school bag, pulls out what seems to be a lot of papers, and puts them on the edge of the table. He sits down and is about to start doing his correcting, but he's cold. So, he decides to put one of his mittens back on and then realizes that he's still very cold and puts on the other mitten. He then tries to pick up his pen, which is very difficult.*

He reaches into his pocket and takes out a small bottle of cognac. He takes a quick swig. It seems to warm him up for an instant. He places it next to him.

There's a knock at the door.

PIERRE *immediately grabs the bottle and puts it away, at the same time causing him to knock over all the copies that he had on the table. He frantically starts picking up the copies on the floor.*

There's another knock on the door.)

PIERRE. *(Shouts.)* Come in.

(The door opens and GEORGETTE enters. GEORGETTE is what people used to call a solid woman. She's a good ten years older than PIERRE. Slightly heavy and speaks rather loudly. She is somewhat straightforward. However, she is intimidated by the surroundings.)

GEORGETTE. Bonjour, Monsieur.
PIERRE. Bonjour. *(She looks at all the papers that are now on the floor. She's a little hesitant, then looks at him strangely, realizing that he is wearing his overcoat over what seems to be part of a smock.*

PIERRE manages to gather all of his papers and finally gathers his courage as well.) Yes?

GEORGETTE. I'm awfully sorry to disturb you but I'm looking for a Monsieur ... ah, I always forget his name. The students call him Carrot-face.

PIERRE. Oh, you probably mean Monsieur Gustave Bémont. He's the gentleman who shares this laboratory with me.

GEORGETTE. He's not here?

PIERRE. Oh, it shouldn't be too long.

GEORGETTE. I can wait.

(She immediately makes herself at home and sits down.)

PIERRE. I guess you can. Although, if you want to stay warm, you'd probably be better off outside.

GEORGETTE. *(Laughs,)* Yes, I agree. A person could freeze their asses in here.

PIERRE. Well, that's one way of putting it, Miss ...?

GEORGETTE. Georgette.

PIERRE. Georgette. Incidentally, I don't think you should call Mousier Bémont, Carrot-face.

GEORGETTE. Oh, I don't call him that. Everybody else does.

PIERRE. Ah, yes, well, you know how it is ... students like to give their teachers nicknames.

GEORGETTE. And what's your nickname?

PIERRE. Well, as far as I know, I don't have one. My name is Curie. Pierre Curie.

GEORGETTE. Yes, of course. We know each other.

PIERRE. We do?

GEORGETTE. I'm the waitress at Chez Georgine. You don't recognize me?

PIERRE. You own it?

GEORGETTE. No, no, no. I'm Georgette. That's Georgine.

PIERRE. I do go there occasionally.

GEORGETTE. You once dropped an entire bowl of pea soup on my legs.

PIERRE. I did? Oh, I'm so sorry. I guess I am somewhat awkward that way. As a matter of fact you might say I'm the master of awkwardness.

GEORGETTE. You're not awkward you're just distracted, that's all. Like all geniuses.

PIERRE. I am not a genius, I assure you. I'm simply doing my work which is research in physics and chemistry ... just like Monsieur Bémont.

GEORGETTE. Anyway, I'm sure that when you're at your work you don't make awkward mistakes.

PIERRE. No. Luckily I do not. *(He sits down, and unfortunately doesn't quite sit properly and knocks the chair which goes flying. He grabs it, and in doing so, manages somehow to knock all his paperwork once again on the floor.)* Damnit. *(GEORGETTE immediately goes to help him, getting down on her knees.)* No, please. Leave it. I beg of you. *(She starts grabbing some of his papers.)* Please, please ... this is most embarrassing to me.

GEORGETTE. Oh, no, it's an honor for me to be helping you. You're involved in such interesting work.

PIERRE. Why thank you. Science, when it's pure, can in fact be a very noble endeavor.

GEORGETTE. Is it true what they say, that you people in here are always working with all kinds of bottles and tubes and changing things from orange to blue and making noises like bloop, bloops and gloop, gloops?

PIERRE. Well, let's just say that, occasionally, we are involved in some rather spectacular experiments.

GEORGETTE. *(Excitedly.)* Would you consider demonstrating something that jumps or explodes, even a little bit?

PIERRE. I really must ask you to excuse me but I have all these copies to correct ....

GEORGETTE. Oh, please, do something that becomes ... all red.

PIERRE. I'm afraid I'm the one who's going to become all red if you get me angry.

(The front door opens and GUSTAVE BÉMONT enters. Sure enough, he has a thick reddish beard as well as red hair. He is a contemporary of PIERRE's.)

BÉMONT. Bonjour, Pierre.

PIERRE. Oh, Gustave. Bonjour.

BÉMONT. Still no coal?

PIERRE. Oh, they said it won't be long now. Just an administrative mix-up.

GEORGETTE. Exactly.

PIERRE. Oh, there's this person who wishes to see you.

(BÉMONT, recognizing GEORGETTE, quickly goes to her.)

BÉMONT. Mademoiselle Georgette, you here?

GEORGETTE. Yes, Monsieur Carrot – fa –, I mean, Bémont. You always leave me a nice tip at the restaurant and you always have a nice word for me, and since I have such respect for geniuses ... like yourselves.... Anyway, I came here to tell you ....

(She hesitates.)

BÉMONT. What? *(GEORGETTE looks back and forth at both of them.)* WHAT?

GEORGETTE. Well, the directeur of this school is a rather large gentleman they call Chevrier?

BÉMONT. Yes, the directeur of the school of physics and chemistry is effectively Rodolphe Chevrier. And, yes, he's rather corpulent.

GEORGETTE. He has an associate by the name of Baudet ... Bolet ... Bonet?

BÉMONT. Binèt.

GEORGETTE. That's it. Binèt.

BÉMONT. Yes, Professor Binèt. The titular head of the Chair of Anatomy here at the Sorbonne, and definitely a good friend of Monsieur Chevrier.

GEORGETTE. Well, the other day Chevrier was complaining to this Binèt person about you and Monsieur Curie.

BÉMONT. I don't believe you.

GEORGETTE. I swear. He was telling him that you two are just not inventing enough ... things. And Binèt said to him, "Well, all you have to do is cut their coal supply." And Chevrier thought that was the funniest idea he had ever heard.

PIERRE. You must be mistaken.

GEORGETTE. No, no, I'm not mistaken. In fact, he told him, "You're absolutely right. If they don't start working and getting something done, their lab is going to become the 'rendezvous of polar bears. A Pavilion for Eskimos.'"

BÉMONT. He said that?

GEORGETTE. They laughed and laughed. And I think it's just awful letting minds like yours freeze their asses off.

BÉMONT. A Pavilion for Eskimos.

PIERRE. I, I just can't believe it. I know that Chevrier is very demanding but still ....

GEORGETTE. Just like my uncle up until he married my aunt, always laughing, always having a good time. And then six months after they were married he goes and cuts off her finger because she was biting her nails.

PIERRE. Are you sure that's what you heard them say?

GEORGETTE. Word for word. *(She raises her hand and spits in it.)* I swear.

(PIERRE and BÉMONT are a little taken aback by the spitting.)

PIERRE. Yes, well, thank you very much ... and if you don't mind, we really have to get back to work now.

GEORGETTE. I beg your pardon.

PIERRE. Monsieur Bémont and I have things to talk about.

GEORGETTE. *(Realizing.)* Oh, I'm sorry. I'm going. But some-day you promise to make those gloop, gloop noises for me?

PIERRE. *(A little embarrassed.)* Ah, yes, someday.

BÉMONT. Au revoir. Thank you.

PIERRE. Au revoir.

(GEORGETTE opens the door, starts to go, stops and turns.)

GEORGETTE. *(Calls out to them.)* We have pig's feet for lunch today. Should I put some aside for you?

PIERRE. No, thank you.

BÉMONT. Well, maybe a little ....

GEORGETTE. *(Muttering to herself as she goes.)* Well, maybe a little. What is that supposed to mean?

(She exits.)

PIERRE. You believe her?

BÉMONT. And you don't?

PIERRE. Well, she seems a little excitable, and besides, it's so undignified of Chevrier.

BÉMONT. Well then, where's the coal?

PIERRE. I imagine the school is short on coal these days.

BÉMONT. In that case, that would mean that everyone is freezing all over the school, correct?

PIERRE. Yes, I suppose.

BÉMONT. Well, I'm going to go find out.

(He quickly exits with determination. PIERRE remains there alone. He shrugs, goes back to his table, sits down and waits a moment. Then, to himself:)

PIERRE. The rendezvous of polar bears.

(PIERRE accidentally hits his elbow against his stack of papers and once again everything goes flying on the floor. He picks up everything, mutters to himself, puts everything back on the table and starts quickly to correct his papers. He's moving at an incredibly rapid pace, seemingly annoyed by everything that has just taken place.
All of a sudden, the door opens and BÉMONT reenters carrying a wooden chair, which has a cushion.)

BÉMONT. There is coal everywhere except here. The amphitheater, the hall, Monsieur Chevrier's office. It's warm everywhere except here. *(He goes over to the stove and inhales deeply.)* Our stove has actually been sprayed with water. Do you need any more proof?

PIERRE. I can't believe it.

BÉMONT. Now he's gone too far.

PIERRE. We don't produce enough?

BÉMONT. That man is impossible. He's just like his colleague, Binèt. All they care about is submitting our research papers to the Academy, in the hopes of landing some sort of prize or honor. Something to enhance their stature among their peers. We work, they get the credit. It's quite a system.

PIERRE. We can't invent at will. We're not magicians who pull rabbits out of their sleeves. I don't know what's the matter with people today. Everyone has this music hall mentality.

BÉMONT. Very well then, what we're going to do is heat our stove with wood. I took this from Chevrier's secretary. *(BÉMONT begins breaking apart the wooden chair. He rips the cushion apart and starts filling the stove with material and pieces of wood. He then adds to it the contents of a small pharmaceutical carafe and proceeds to fan the fire. We suddenly see some light coming from inside the stove and the two of them warm their hands over it.)* I have had it up to here with that big oaf. He had better give us some coal or else I'm going to rearrange his entire face.

PIERRE. Oh sure, have yourself dismissed. That would help a great deal.

BÉMONT. Not only do we have to work like fiends with those students, we also have to do research that produces laurels for the school, so that he can sit comfortably in his office, his feet on his desk and his fingers massaging that fat belly of his, with the hopes of someday being elected to the Academy of Sciences.

PIERRE. I'm completely in accord with you but don't overreact. If you remember correctly, he once thought of letting you go. It's not something that you should be pursuing right now.

BÉMONT. Believe me, it's just a matter of time before my inventions allow me to slam the door in his face.

PIERRE. Apropos, where are you with the uh … the uh …?

BÉMONT. The acoustiphone?

PIERRE. Yes, exactly, the Bémont acoustiphone. Where are you with it?

BÉMONT. The project is presently being examined. Nobody seems to question the ingenuity of the system, nor the improvement of the very crisp sound that it produces, but the brass cork seems to be causing certain frightened businessmen to hesitate.

(He goes to an armoire and pulls out this rather bizarre contraption and looks at it proudly.)

PIERRE. Well, you're still hopeful, are you not?

BÉMONT. Of course. All I need is a little pressure from those who are in need of my invention. In other words, I have to be heard by the deaf.

PIERRE. Write to them.

BÉMONT. When I think of you and your quartz electrometer. You're sitting on gold, I tell you. You're not even finished with it and you're ready to put it into the public domain.

PIERRE. Please, let's not start.

BÉMONT. Just like you did with your aperiodique scale and your optic objective. Both of which are filling the pockets of industrialists.

PIERRE. Yes, and because of that, the apparatus is being utilized, at a very low cost, by other scientists throughout the world.

BÉMONT. To work on the same researches as you are and maybe even beat you to it.

PIERRE. Such is the challenge of science.

BÉMONT. Or the naïveté of certain dimwits. Look, we're dealing with bitter international competition ... not a gentlemen's sport. The time to give things away is over.

(He puts his apparatus carefully into the armoire.)

PIERRE. Well, in that case why waste our time inventing trivialities instead of working on more ambitious, finer discoveries?

BÉMONT. You call the acoustiphone a trivial invention?

PIERRE. Well ... I don't say that it's totally useless, but it does play a minor role compared to uh ... oh, I don't know ... let's say, the structure of matter. You know what Pasteur said, "The scientist who allows himself to be tempted by practical applications complicates his life and paralyzes in himself all hopes of discovery."

BÉMONT. Pasteur never misses an opportunity to babble, does

he? The pasteurization of milk, the vaccine against rabies, the amelioration of Brewer's yeast for beers ... are those not practical applications?

PIERRE. In any case, the very idea of gain is detrimental to science.

BÉMONT. And the extra labor, the humiliation, the lack of proper equipment ... who do they benefit?

PIERRE. I didn't say that.

BÉMONT. And our miserable salaries ... are they necessary too?

PIERRE. Poverty never bothered me.

BÉMONT. Yes, till you get married.

PIERRE. I won't get married.

BÉMONT. You mean now you're renouncing women too?

PIERRE. I've thought about it a great deal. Those charming creatures have the best reasons in the world to distract us from our work. Family, the instinct of the nest, maternity. But one has to be cautious.

BÉMONT. Cautious?

PIERRE. Women have no place in my life.

BÉMONT. Have you gone completely mad?

PIERRE. I am as sane as the next fellow.

BÉMONT. Aren't you attracted to women?

PIERRE. I simply put an "X" through that question and you should do likewise.

BÉMONT. Me? Now I know you're mad.

PIERRE. I'm telling you this for your own good. Women are disastrous to a scientific career.

BÉMONT. They're my reason for living. Renounce women? Those celestial, blissful creatures. Why, only last week during Offenbach's "La Belle Hèlenè," in the third scene, there was a creature, I'm not quite sure what muse she was ... she was dressed in at least half a pound of grapes. Ah, but what a sight! How can you not see in all women a nymph ready to moan with drunkenness. Every day in the trolley, I, I don't know how I'm able to restrain myself from, literally, ripping off their dresses between the Rue Madeleine and the Boulevard Caumartin.

PIERRE. I never go to the opera and I walk to work. One has to know how to avoid temptation.

BÉMONT. You're living like a monk. Completely out of step with the times.

PIERRE. Not at all.

BÉMONT. What are your pleasures?

PIERRE. My pleasures?

BÉMONT. Yes, your pleasures.

PIERRE. Well, there are many. Reading.

BÉMONT. What have you read recently?

PIERRE. Well … recently. Uh, recently?

BÉMONT. Or seen? Or done?

PIERRE. Well, it's true that recently ….

BÉMONT. You don't know anything that's going on, do you? What if I mentioned Toulouse Lautrec?

PIERRE. A new train line?

BÉMONT. Alright, how about uh … who is the President of the Republic right now?

PIERRE. Please, let's not be ridiculous.

BÉMONT. Go ahead, tell me his name.

PIERRE. Well, uh, let's see … Carnot?

BÉMONT. Yes. Correct.

PIERRE. Henri Carnot. Even more correct.

BÉMONT. Henri? Henri Carnot? Sadi Carnot, you blockhead.

PIERRE. Well, I was close.

BÉMONT. Admit it. You are only interested in science. The rest of it, you couldn't care less.

PIERRE. Well … I guess you're not completely wrong.

BÉMONT. Then fight for your rights so that they will, at least, respect you. Here you are given no consideration, without materials with which to experiment. Me? I'm ready to revolt. I'm nowhere as good as you are, but I'm trying to find a way to finance my own re- searches. You, you're going to remain under the thumb of that fat ty- rannical swine …. *(CHEVRIER enters. He's wearing an impressive long coat. He's about fifty.)* That Herr … Chevrier.

CHEVRIER. *(Dryly.)* Bonjour, Bémont. Bonjour, Curie.

PIERRE. Bonjour, Herr … Monsieur Chevrier.

CHEVRIER. So the work … it's progressing?

BÉMONT. Every day.

CHEVRIER. We can expect some sort of written communiqué?

BÉMONT. I am almost at the point of discovery.

CHEVRIER. And you, Curie. Your famous quartz electrometer?

PIERRE. I'm afraid I've reached an impasse, Monsieur Chevrier.

CHEVRIER. Impasse? What do you mean by impasse?

PIERRE. It seems to function perfectly with all metals except for one.

CHEVRIER. Which one?

PIERRE. Uranium. With uranium, my electrometer goes completely out of kilter.

CHEVRIER. Out of kilter? Really?

PIERRE. It seems to measure more current than it is fed.

CHEVRIER. Which of course is impossible.

PIERRE. Exactly.

CHEVRIER. And what do you attribute this to?

PIERRE. I would say to a hidden snag in my apparatus.

CHEVRIER. Which one?

PIERRE. Precisely. That's what I'm looking for.

CHEVRIER. Well then, find it. The state pays you to find not to look.

PIERRE. I'm afraid teaching is monopolizing most of my time.

CHEVRIER. Yes, that's why it's called "teaching." As for your apparatus … either you resolve the problem and write your research paper or you give up and submit the problem to the Academy. You have spun your wheels long enough.

PIERRE. I don't need any help, Monsieur Chevrier. I will find the problem.

CHEVRIER. Very well, then let us move on to something else. You, Bémont, can I see your experimental notes on the spectros copier?

BÉMONT. My notes? Well, uh … I don't think you'll learn anything from them. And may I respectfully remind you that I have the greatest need for a more perfected interferometer.

CHEVRIER, Materials. Always materials. It's the same story over and over again.

BÉMONT. One cannot envision grand discoveries without proper materials.

CHEVRIER. Oh, really? What about Copernicus? And Galileo? And Newton? A simple apple and boom, Universal Gravitation! Two centuries later we're still talking about it. Now, if you want apples or pears, I can have them deliver you crates full.

BÉMONT. Some coal would be appreciated. Haven't you noticed the temperature in this laboratory?

CHEVRIER. Yes. I would say it's ideal.

BÉMONT. The cold air is affecting our apparati.

CHEVRIER. Maybe, but it invigorates the brain.

PIERRE. Monsieur Chevrier, I'm afraid that what you say is a physiological counter-truth. Under a certain temperature the cold actually causes sleep.

CHEVRIER. How bizarre. And I was just starting to warm up.

BÉMONT. I wouldn't want to be the one to spread malicious gossip ... but it would appear that you are cutting our coal supply.

CHEVRIER. Absolutely! I *am* cutting your coal supply because you are sabotaging my efforts to elevate this school in the eyes of the Academy. You seem to forget, this is France!

PIERRE. Sabotaging?

CHEVRIER. Yes, you, Curie. You waste your time with sterile inventions ... maybe ingenious, but for which the world, outside of a few laboratory rats, couldn't care less. As for you, Bémont, you must take me for an imbecile.

BÉMONT. Pardon?

CHEVRIER. You spend hours on clandestine laboratory research for personal profit ...

BÉMONT. Who told you such nonsense?

CHEVRIER. Who? My dear Bémont, not a week goes by without some industrialist writing me, demanding to know how some professor, who goes around demonstrating some acoustic gadget, is capable of finding time to teach physics and chemistry to our young elite. It's scandalous enough that you fleece the school ... but to discredit it as well.

BÉMONT. With your permission I'd like to make a point.

CHEVRIER. No! I didn't come here to have a discussion with you, I came here to tell you two things. Primo: you have exactly one month and one bucket of coal to turn over, both of you, a research paper destined for the Academy, clearly outlining your work. Secundo: I am bringing in some reinforcements.

BÉMONT. Reinforcements?

CHEVRIER. Precisely. Since both of you are not up to the task … this morning I am awaiting a young Polish student whose name is … *(He looks at his piece of paper.)* Sklo … Dow … Ska. Who apparently doesn't speak our language, which, of course, renders her unqualified to teach. However, she is ladened with diplomas, relentless they say, and anxious to work in a laboratory. I expect a great deal from this young person. It's unbelievable to me having to import strangers to work in France doing the work that the French no longer wish to do.

BÉMONT. Three? We are going to be three in here?

CHEVRIER. Yes, and within a few moments. Which should give you just enough time to assure me, that given her sex, you're not going to involve her in any of those stupid university hazings. If so … start packing.

PIERRE. Yes, that's really our style.

CHEVRIER. You, I don't know. *(He looks at BÉMONT.)* But *him*, just look at him. I don't want to take a chance.

PIERRE. But three people working on the same apparati, don't we risk to be even *less* productive?

CHEVRIER. Maybe. In which case we'll soon find out which of the three is superfluous. In the meantime, I'll see about the coal.

(CHEVRIER exits.)

BÉMONT. And there we are, once again humiliated, disparaged, and diminished.

PIERRE. I have to be honest, I almost lost my temper.

BÉMONT. You notice, I'm always the one to get into trouble. I had to be the one to bring up the coal. You … not a word.

PIERRE. Well, you have to admit it doesn't look good. Your collaborating with industry, that's what's giving him an ulcer. You shouldn't be mixing school with business.

BÉMONT. How else am I supposed to get proper credit for my inventions?

PIERRE. Not only are we going to be more cramped in here ... but with a woman, to boot.

BÉMONT. Well, maybe she's ... delectable.

PIERRE. That's enough. *(There's a knock at the door. PIERRE indicates the chair to BÉMONT.)* Sit down. Sit. *(BÉMONT sits. PIERRE calls out.)* Come in. *(MARIE SKLODOWSKA, early twenties, carrying a bucket of coal, enters. She's wearing a black dress, black hat, black coat. Her hair is pulled back in a bun. She wears glasses. She is the absolute image of austerity. A moment passes. BÉMONT is still seated. PIERRE goes to her, takes the bucket of coal, passes it to BÉMONT and begins speaking to her in a rather loud and deliberate tone. BÉMONT takes the coal and puts a few pieces in the stove.)* Come in. You are Mademoiselle ...?

MARIE. *(She speaks with a slight East European accent.)* Sklodowska.

PIERRE. Mademoiselle Sklo ... dowska. When Professeur Chevrier told us about your arrival we were at first, I hasten to say, a little bit hostile. Maybe he told you about it. However, upon reflection, scientific solidarity obliges us to make of a misfortune, good fortune. So that even if the installations here are modest and even if your arrival poses certain difficulties, may I welcome you to the laboratory. My name is Pierre Curie and this is Monsieur Gustave Bémont.

MARIE. Please ... to speak ... more ... slow?

PIERRE. Do you speak Spanish?

MARIE. No ... speak ... no.

PIERRE. Sprechen sie Deutsch?

MARIE. Jawohl!

PIERRE. Yes, well I don't. *(To BÉMONT.)* Do you?

BÉMONT. No.

(MARIE looks through her small portable dictionary.)

MARIE. *(With deliberation.)* I am good happiness to make acquaintances.

PIERRE. And we are too, Mademoiselle.

MARIE. *(Her nose in the dictionary, indicating the table.)* At what hour is the next explosion? *(PIERRE and BÉMONT look at each other, suppress a laugh. She indicates the table.)* It is permitted to camp here?

PIERRE. But of course.

(He quickly pushes things aside on the table, taking over more of BÉ-MONT's area than his own. BÉMONT, seeing this, tries to rearrange things to his advantage. PIERRE attempts to make it more equitable. He manages to drop several things on the floor, which, of course, he retrieves awkwardly.

In the meantime, MARIE is quickly going through her dictionary looking to utter her next phrase.)

MARIE. *(Indicating the coat rack.)* Possibility for student Sklodowska to hanging coat on your thing?

(BÉMONT starts to laugh. PIERRE has a lot of difficulty holding back his laughter.)

PIERRE. Yes, but we call it a coat rack.

MARIE. Oh. Coat rack. Yes, better than your thing.

BÉMONT. Better, but not as funny.

MARIE. Coat hanger. Thank you. Student Sklodowska will remember.

(BÉMONT grabs a piece of paper off the desk and goes over to PIERRE, pointing to it and pretending to be talking about something.)

BÉMONT. Well, she's not exactly one of the can-can dancers at the Moulin Rouge ... but I have the feeling we might be able to have a few laughs with her. Especially if she doesn't speak the language. Look at her. Some fashion plate. She looks like one of those widows in Brittany off to dig for mussels.

PIERRE. *(Not having the nerve to speak in front of MARIE, whether she understands or not.)* Yes, these elements are isotopes, beryllium, fluorescences, aluminum.

(In the meantime MARIE has hung up her coat, sharpened her pencil,

taken a few things out of her bag.)

MARIE. Student Sklodowska possibility use potentiometer for work asked by the Chevrier professeur?

PIERRE. Certainly.

BÉMONT. How long? I'm actually going to need the potentiometer. May I see your research papers?

MARIE. Please to speak much more slow.

(BÉMONT takes the paper from her and reads:)

BÉMONT. "Spectroanalysis and study of the atomic structure of non-steel metals." But … Chevrier gave her the same assignment he gave me. He doesn't trust me?

(BÉMONT shows the paper to PIERRE.)

PIERRE. Let me see. Oh, you're correct. Unquestionably.

BÉMONT. Well now, my friend, he has gone too far. I don't give a damn anymore. If he wants to just sit on my discoveries that's up to him. I'm going to find him. It's her or me. Chevrier will have to make the decision.

PIERRE. No, wait. I'll intercede. I'll tell Chevrier to find her another research project.

BÉMONT. Too late. Anyway we'd only be at each other's throats. Grabbing each other's apparatus. No. I've made up my mind. It's either *her* or *me.*

(BÉMONT rushes towards the door. MARIE suddenly moves like lightning and rushes to the door before him and stands there defiantly, menacing, to rip her blouse.)

MARIE. *(Suddenly able to speak the language perfectly but with her slight East European accent.)* You listen to me and listen well, you simpleton. I drudged in Poland for ten years as a nanny, just to pay for my studies. I wheeled and schemed like an animal so that I could continue those studies in France. I worked myself to the bones to get this job. So, I'm certainly not going to take a chance, having just gotten here, and allow a psychopathic runt like you, stir up shit with the headmaster. *(PIERRE and BÉMONT can't believe their ears. She continues.)* If either of you makes one move towards me, I rip my blouse, I scratch myself, and I scream rape. This is not a joke. I can cry on cue. I will accuse both of you ... and they'll believe me. I once did it in Poland to a Russian officer. He's presently in Siberia, laying down rail tracks without gloves.

(BÉMONT makes a slight move. MARIE immediately starts ripping her collar. He stops himself.)

BÉMONT. *(To PIERRE.)* She has me. I once had a problem with the police. I had a scuffle in a closet with a husband.
PIERRE. But we can't give in to blackmail.
MARIE. All I am asking is to stay. I'll make it easy for everybody. Chevrier will give me the same research as you. If you want, I find nothing. If you want, I help you and you sign your names to the research papers. I'll work fastidiously. I'll do the cleaning, everything. On the condition that I am accepted here.
BÉMONT. *(Making a step towards her.)* But first ...
MARIE. *(Screaming.)* Rape!

(BÉMONT immediately backs off and then, a moment later, continues.)

BÉMONT. Why were you pretending not to speak the language before?
MARIE. So that you could speak freely, which of course is what you did. Thank you very much for the Brittany widow digging for mussels.
BÉMONT. Yes, and hanging your coat on our "thing," that's real distinguished.
MARIE. Well, it served a purpose. I could see you were starting to make a list of all my mistakes. It gave me a certain je ne sais quoi.
PIERRE. What duplicity!
MARIE. "It is the results that matter." To quote Lucrecia Borgia.

I wish to stay!

(The door opens and CHEVRIER enters.)

CHEVRIER. Is this where the cry of rape came from? Well, Bémont? Is it?

BÉMONT. I, I didn't hear anything, Monsieur Le Directeur.

CHEVRIER. Everything is going well?

BÉMONT. Just uh … marvelous.

CHEVRIER. *(To MARIE.)* And you? Is everything the way you wish it?

MARIE. *(Smiling timidly.)* Please to speak more slow.

CHEVRIER. Yes, well, it must be those idiot students again.

(He rushes out. A moment passes and then BÉMONT begins to laugh softly.)

BÉMONT. Well, I've been had. You have unquestionably left me speechless. *(He laughs a little more.)* All in all I must admit that I prefer you like this. And the disguise, is that part of the sleight of hand also?

MARIE. Obviously. I'm not here to seduce a bunch of medical students with frills and petticoats. In order to cross the ocean of obscenity that exists in this masculine science, occasionally one has to wear the equivalent of a diving suit.

PIERRE. I can't believe what I'm hearing.

BÉMONT. Well, you can't reproach her for being realistic.

PIERRE. You mean super cynical.

MARIE. I swear I can be of some use to you.

BÉMONT. As a matter of fact, you can. It so happens … do you see those calculations over there? They really need to be verified while I go write up a patent.

MARIE. Gladly. A patent for what, if I may be so indiscreet?

BÉMONT. Well, actually, it's not for the school.

MARIE. That's quite alright.

BÉMONT. It's a patent for an acoustic apparatus for the deaf. I've been asked to develop this project.

MARIE. Fascinating. It sounds like a grand idea.

BÉMONT. *(To PIERRE.)* Are you listening?

MARIE. A residence amplification system.

BÉMONT. Exactly.

MARIE. Destined to be produced commercially?

BÉMONT. But of course.

MARIE. How much might one stand to gain financially from such an apparatus?

BÉMONT. Oh, it could be quite substantial.

MARIE. And how does one go about obtaining … a patent?

BÉMONT. You're interested?

MARIE. Oh, just to know.

BÉMONT. You have a project?

MARIE. Ah, no … not really. What exactly can one patent?

BÉMONT. Everything. An apparatus, a system, a box opener, even the formula to a perfume. That's how Louis Pivel made his fortune. Inventing a synthetic perfume.

(A beat.)

MARIE. The formula for an alcohol that leaves you without a hangover, could that be patented?

BÉMONT. *(Lighting up.)* Patented … that could be worth a fortune.

MARIE. It exists. My great, great grandfather discovered it. It's a vodka in which you steep seven different herbs in different quantities. And it's impossible to get sick.

BÉMONT. You're pulling my leg.

MARIE. No, I'm quite serious. I can actually make you some, if you'd like.

BÉMONT. Please.

PIERRE. I can't believe you two. Industry, commerce … where do you think you are?

(We hear the sound of the school alarm in the distance.)

BÉMONT. We must go teach our classes. But I'm very, very interested. We'll talk again a little later.

MARIE. So, I'm accepted?
BÉMONT. Indubitably.
PIERRE. We shall see about that.

(PIERRE and BÉMONT exit. MARIE stays alone. She approaches PIERRE's quartz electrometer on one of the tables. She looks at it with interest and starts cleaning the floor.
Lights fade.)

Scene 2

(Same day. We can see by the pendulum clock that it is now two hours later. It is no longer snowing and it is much clearer outside.
MARIE is seated at a table and is finishing correcting copies left behind by PIERRE.
PIERRE enters. He moves stiffly. He avoids MARIE's glance. He goes to the stove and rubs his hands together. He then removes his overcoat and underneath we see that the white smock is now being worn properly.)

MARIE. Your course went well, Professeur Curie?
PIERRE. *(A little cold, a little impersonal.)* Quite well. I thank you for the inquiry, Mademoiselle Sklodowska.

(After a moment or two, PIERRE comes toward the table.)

MARIE. I hope you don't mind, Professeur Curie, I took the liberty of correcting your copies … with a pencil, of course.

(PIERRE looks through the copies.)

PIERRE. This is very good work
MARIE. Thank you.
PIERRE. However, I'm going to ask you to erase it all.
MARIE. But why?

PIERRE. Because it's not honest. My students have the right to have me be the only judge of their work, That is what I signed up for.

MARIE. But what a waste of time.

PIERRE. Integrity is never a waste of time, nor is honesty. Two cardinal qualities for the scientist, which you seem totally void of.

MARIE. I'm terribly sorry about my arrival this morning. I did wish to tell you how much I admire your work. You're quite well known in Poland.

PIERRE. Yes, sure.

MARIE. Well, it's true. My professeur, Madame Paczula, never stops talking about your work with Piezo electricity.

PIERRE. And earlier, was that the truth too? And before that? So far, three different truths in a single morning. It's a little confusing.

MARIE. *(Indicating the electrometer to PIERRE.)* May I? This apparatus apparently serves to measure the electric currents of very weak intensity that pass through different metals. Consequently, they give an indication of the conductivity of those metals. Shall I continue? *(PIERRE looks on in stunned silence.)* Very well, if you don't want to answer, I can't force you. In which case, I will try to make myself useful by washing the windows, which seem to need it very badly.

(She immediately takes a bottle of ammonia, a rag, and gets up on a chair and begins cleaning the windows. Her back is now turned to PIERRE as she starts to involuntarily wiggle her hips.
At first PIERRE doesn't notice her, his scientific mind is somewhere else. But little by little he does start to notice and finally speaks.)

PIERRE. Uh, Mademoiselle Sklodowska, I image your field of inquiry is probably different from mine … *(MARIE continues to scrub and clean.)* After all you're a woman, I'm a man. You come from an occupied country. I live in a free society. It's quite possible that you couldn't help becoming who you are.

MARIE. *(Her back still to him, dryly.)* If you're saying that the human being is the product of society that creates him and not the opposite … then that's what one calls an evidence or a truism.

PIERRE. It's also what we call a positivist idea.

MARIE. *(Still with her back to him — she stops.)* I am a positivist.

PIERRE. Excuse me?

MARIE. *(Turning around.)* I said, I am a positivist. Maybe you
don't appreciate it but that's what I am.

PIERRE. Sacrébleu! So am I. I would never have thought. So
you're a positivist.

MARIE. *(Turning around.)* Positively.

PIERRE. But you lie so much. Is this another one of your fabrica-
tions?

*(MARIE comes down from her chair and gets a photograph out of her
    bag and hands it to PIERRE.)*

MARIE. This photo was taken last year at the masked ball for the
Association of Franco-Polish Positivists. You see the banner? Look to
the left … that's me.

PIERRE. Tied up in a blanket?

MARIE. That blanket is the Polish flag. I represented Poland
breaking her ties.

*(PIERRE hands photo back. In so doing, he lets go of it before she
    has grabbed it. The photo falls to the floor.)*

PIERRE. Sorry. *(He retrieves it and awkwardly hands it to her.)*
Tell me, what goals are you pursuing through science?

MARIE. To accelerate progress. To contribute to and to help lib-
erate humanity of its chains and of its preconceptions.

PIERRE. What else?

MARIE. To accelerate the abolition of painful work. The ad-
vancement of industry and its techniques. The development of means
of communication. The rise of medicine. The rationalization of agri-
culture. The availability of education to all levels of society. The
elimination of superstitions. Let me see what else ….

PIERRE. Well, as I see it, contrary to the inanities that I uttered a
little while ago … your fate is definitely science. Welcome aboard.
And do me a favor, please don't lie anymore. In this country it's not

necessary.

MARIE. My being able to remain here is hanging by a thread. If the reports to my embassy cease to be favorable ... I will be repatriated immediately and excluded from the scientific world.

PIERRE. Isn't there any way of cutting that thread?

MARIE. None. The only possibility is marriage, marriage of convenience, of course. But that's out of the question. My cousin did that. Her so-called husband became infatuated with her. He violated her in the coach after leaving City Hall. She couldn't even report it. And now they have all kinds of debts. No, I'm afraid that marriage of convenience is too much like playing Russian roulette.

PIERRE. I guess.

MARIE. Can we get back to science? Would you consider showing me how your electrometer functions in detail?

PIERRE. Absolutely. Right now, if you'd like. *(He walks towards the quartz.)* See this? When you turn it on, here, the current passes through this middle bulb ... *(Nothing happens.)* Oh, I forgot to plug it in. *(He goes towards the plug.)* I have to admit, not only am I clumsy ... but on top of everything else I'm terribly ... *(As he puts the plug in he gets an awful shock.)* Ahhhhhhh!

(He falls to his knees. MARIE, very concerned, goes to him.)

MARIE. Professeur Curie!
PIERRE. Dd ... dizzy.

(Blackout.)

Scene 3

(Several days later.
The same lighting as in Scene One. However, now outside, a light winter sun is shining. The clock indicates five minutes to eight in the morning.
BÉMONT enters wearing a different outfit, looking rather dapper and holding a package which seems fairly heavy . He hides it in a

corner. He puts a little bit of coal into the stove. He's satisfied that everything is well. He then goes to one of the tables and looks closely at a demijohn filled with a colorless liquid. He kneels down to have a closer look.

The door opens and MARIE enters, causing him to jump slightly. She is holding a two-handled basket, which also seems to be quite heavy.)

BÉMONT. *(Happy to see her.)* Bonjour, Marie.

MARIE. Bonjour, Gustave.

BÉMONT. So, the work is progressing?

MARIE. Not that well. I'm afraid I've been dragging my feet a little.

BÉMONT. I want you to know that your vodka was *fabulous.* Yesterday I drank and drank till I was dead drunk. I vaguely remember becoming involved in a tap dance contest with La Goulue at the Moulin Rouge. And this morning I woke up fresh as a daisy.

MARIE. I told you.

BÉMONT. I prepared a contract. Fifty fifty. Here, you sign here. Of course, that is if you agree .... *(He takes out a paper. MARIE reads it quickly and signs.)* Now, you have to tell me the recipe, the herbs, the proportions, everything.

MARIE. Did you bring what I asked you to bring?

(BÉMONT gets the parcel with which he entered.)

BÉMONT. Yes, but it wasn't easy. *(He puts the parcel onto the table with a bit of difficulty and starts unwrapping it.)* A bust of Pasteur was simple enough to find .... *(And sure enough it is a bust of Pasteur, made of plaster.)* However, finding one with a head that screws on and off .... *(He demonstrates.)* I had to talk to a lot of artisans. Are you going to tell me what it's for?

MARIE. It's personal. Here's the formula for the vodka.

(She gives him a piece of paper.)

BÉMONT. *(Looking over the paper.)* But all this can be found in any store.

MARIE. Naturally.

BÉMONT. Fantastique. I have some large kegs in my basement. I'm buying everything this afternoon and starting tonight, I let it seep. And in three days ... *(Snaps fingers.)* ... into the bottles. Oh, apropos, I found a good name for it. CHEVRIKAIA. What do you think?

MARIE. It's more Russian than Polish, but why not?

BÉMONT. Now, as to our other project. Have you developed the photos?

MARIE. Yes. The plates are over there along with the proofs. Would you be so kind as to put the Pasteur next to my materials over there?

(BÉMONT immediately takes the Pasteur bust and places it on the other table.)

BÉMONT. *(While doing the above.)* Tell me, are the photographs as ooh, la, la as my uncle led me to believe?

MARIE. That's putting it rather mildly.

BÉMONT. He's quite an original, that old rascal. He spends his entire days taking photographs of living tableaus in his home. I guess he finds it stimulating.

MARIE. In any event, he pays well.

BÉMONT. Needless to say he's very grateful that he doesn't have to have these developed commercially. *(He looks at some of the proof sheets and reacts.)* Oh, my God. This is squarely pornographic.

MARIE. Yes. And you'll notice I had to adjust some of the contrasts.

BÉMONT. You're not shocked?

MARIE. The scientific eye shocks at nothing.

BÉMONT. Oh, good, because I have another series.

MARIE. Same price?

BÉMONT. Same price.

MARIE. *(Holds out her hand.)* Give.

(BÉMONT gives her some new photo plates. We hear the general sound of the school alarm.)

BÉMONT. I have to run. I'll be back around ten. Good luck

(He quickly exits.
MARIE goes to her basket and pulls out a large pot, which she places on the gas stove with great effort. She lights it, looks inside it, and then closes the lid. She also takes out of her basket a package of powder which she begins to mix into a crucible along with another powder.
PIERRE enters, all smiles.)

PIERRE. Bonjour, Marie.

MARIE. *(Taken aback.)* Bonjour, Pierre.

PIERRE. Well then, how are we doing with our project on this most beautiful of all possible days?

MARIE. I finished verifying all your measurements. Everything is perfect. And yet, with the uranium, your apparatus indicates certain electrical qualities that are completely extraordinary.

PIERRE. Damn it. It's inexplicable. Let me see your notes.

(MARIE shows him her notes. The two of them lean in. PIERRE, unconsciously, puts his arm on MARIE's shoulder. She immediately recoils.)

MARIE. Professeur Curie, just because you had the kindness to marry me does not mean you can take certain liberties.

PIERRE. Oh, I'm so sorry ....

MARIE. We agreed it was strictly out of convenience. You were lending a helping hand to a fellow scientist.

PIERRE. Absolutely. You know, I think we're going to have to completely rethink our approach with other materials. *(Reacting, he continues.)* What do I smell?

(PIERRE approaches the boiling pot and removes the cover.)

MARIE. Goulash! It's a Polish holiday tomorrow and my sister is in charge of bringing the national dish. It has to simmer for twenty-four hours.

PIERRE. Which reminds me ... dzisiaj wieczorem papuga zygfryd usiadzie dwa razy na aperze bez placenia.

MARIE. *(Thrilled.)* Tsou dovnie. Where did you learn that?

PIERRE. *(Taking out a conversation manual.)* I have thrown myself wholeheartedly into the Polish language.

MARIE. You composed that phrase all by yourself?

PIERRE. Yes. Is it correct?

MARIE. Absolutely.

PIERRE. And the pronunciation?

MARIE. Almost perfect. *(She then proceeds to say it more correctly.)* Dzisiaj wieczorem papuga zygfryd usiadzie dwa razy no operze bez placenia. Tonight, Siegfried, the parakeet, sits twice on the opera without paying.

PIERRE. But that's not at all what I wanted to say.

MARIE. What did you want to say?

PIERRE. Tonight, for the performance of the opera, "Siegfried," I have two free tickets.

MARIE. Yes, that is a little different.

PIERRE. Well, will you accompany me?

MARIE. Oh, thank you so very much, really, but Wagner is very hard on my ears. I'm sure you'll find someone who will be most happy to go with you.

PIERRE. But it's you that I'd like to make happy. *(He tries to pull her towards him. She immediately kicks him in the shin. He starts to dance around the laboratory in tremendous pain.)* I'm sorry. I don't know what came over me. *(He notices the demijohn of vodka.)* I'm going to have to tell Gustave to get rid of this concoction. *(He examines the photo proofs and suddenly reacts.)* Oh, my God ... what horrible student had the nerve to deposit this filth in our lab? I hope you didn't see this.

MARIE. Gustave is the one who gives them to me to develop so that I can earn extra money.

PIERRE. *(Astonished.)* I can't believe my ears. And that ...? *(He indicates the bust of Pasteur and its separated head along with the mix of powders in the crucible.)* ... and that?

MARIE. You promise not to tell anyone?

PIERRE. I promise nothing.

MARIE. Not if you don't promise.

PIERRE. Very well, I promise.

MARIE. *(Indicating the bust of Pasteur.)* It's for a clandestine operation ... for the Polish resistance here in Paris.

PIERRE. What?!!!

MARIE. *(Showing him the powder.)* The dynamite that I'm making.

PIERRE. But you're completely mad. What if somebody saw this?

(CHEVRIER enters.)

CHEVRIER. *(Overly pleasant.)* My dear, Curie, I have been thinking that perhaps I've been a little too harsh on my all-important research scientists. *(Nods to MARIE.)* Mademoiselle ... Mirovska. *(MARIE gives him a very abrupt smile.)* I was telling my associate, Professor Binèt last evening, how you were getting ready to write a research paper on the merits of your electrometer.

PIERRE. Well, not just yet.

CHEVRIER. Surely you're ready for a small private demonstration.

PIERRE. Well, actually, it's not quite ready yet. You see ....

CHEVRIER. Please be reassured that you can count on my total discretion.

PIERRE. I wouldn't want to take up any of your time ....

CHEVRIER. I have nothing but time.

PIERRE. Very well. This way. *(During the following description and explanation, MARIE discreetly hides her photoplaques in the armoire. She turns off the gas under the "goulash." She throws a rag over the demijohn of vodka and quietly replaces the head on the Pasteur bust. PIERRE occasionally looks in her direction. CHEVRIER notices this every now and then, but continues listening to PIERRE.)* Here, Monsieur Chevrier, is the electrometer based, as you know, on the principle of Piezo electricity. A principle from which certain crystals such as quartz are subject to pressure, becoming positively charged at one end and negatively charged at the other. When an electric current is communicated to the electrometer, we can estimate the intensity by measuring the pressure one has to exert on the quartz in order to produce a counter-current of compensation. Like so ....

CHEVRIER. And what is the goal of this apparatus? I mean, concretely.

PIERRE. To measure the exactitude of electrical currents, no matter how weak the intensity.

CHEVRIER. Well, I wouldn't waste too much time with this.

PIERRE. What do you mean?

CHEVRIER. In an age where industry produces and consumes electricity by millions of kilowatts, what is the point of being able to measure infinitesimal tensions? It's as if you were proposing to weigh the coal in that bucket to the tenth of a milligram. There's something a little silly in that, don't you agree?

PIERRE. Ah, but with your permission ....

(At this moment CHEVRIER turns around to face the rest of the laboratory just as MARIE finishes screwing on the head of Pasteur. The head, unfortunately, is turned towards the left of the bust and will remain in this position till the end of the scene.)

CHEVRIER. What else are you cooking up these days? For example, that ... what is that?

(He lifts the rag over the demijohn.)

PIERRE. *(Quickly.)* Oh, this. Oh, this has nothing to do with our work. It so happens that I have an ... intestinal infection and that this mineral water, which comes from a source in the Pyrénées, is most therapeutic. I drink two large glasses every morning.

CHEVRIER. Why in the laboratory? Why not at home?

PIERRE. Because uh ... well, because it has to be very precise. I have to drink my two glasses at nine o'clock exactly. If I don't, it's not as effective, they say.

CHEVRIER. It's true that organisms have always had their own little mysteries. *(He indicates the "goulash.")* And this?

PIERRE. Well, this is ... what it is is ... that is, it's ... it's called ragout of Sulfite of Polandrate, cultivated in the anaerobic fashion.

CHEVRIER. And what is its application?

PIERRE. Well, it's .... In order to artificially produce certain chemicals ... uh ... nutrients ... destined for the animals in the field ....

CHEVRIER. Now, that's something interesting. *(He approaches and inhales the vapors.)* It smells awful. But then again if it's for animals.... Anyway, it shows promise.

PIERRE. Doesn't it? Getting back to my electrometer ....

(Suddenly the clock rings nine.)

CHEVRIER. Nine o'clock already. Well, I guess it's time for your mineral water.

PIERRE. Oh, yes. Thank you. So, as I was saying about my quartz ....

CHEVRIER. No, please ... you have to cure yourself. You have to stay fit to do your research. If you were told nine o'clock precisely then you must drink your water at nine o'clock.

PIERRE. *(Smiles awkwardly.)* Well, a few minutes is not going to matter ....

CHEVRIER. That's what people say and then they forget.

PIERRE. But I assure you that ....

CHEVRIER. *(Suddenly very fatherly.)* Drink your water. It's an order. I don't want to be responsible for your colon.

PIERRE. Very well. So be it.

(He pours himself a glass full of vodka. He hesitates a moment then begins to drink. He starts to choke and cough.)

CHEVRIER. It tastes bad?

PIERRE. *(His voice having been altered.)* Ah-hoo, ah, ah-hoo, ah, ah-ha, ooh, I mean, ah, one has to get used to it.

CHEVRIER. Some of those mineral waters are not very pleasant. But, have courage. *(PIERRE finishes the rest of the glass and seems relieved that that's the end of it.)* Now for the second glass.

(PIERRE can't imagine how he's going to be able to do this. He takes

the second glass and in one swallow finishes the entire contents.)

PIERRE. The ... second glass seemed to go much better. Curious, isn't it?

(H suddenly sways for a moment, but redresses himself.)

CHEVRIER. *(Pointing to the dynamite.)* And this, what is this?
PIERRE. Oh, this is dynoslavomite of the fanaticite. Mademoiselle Sklodowska is in charge of this preparation, which someday might make quite a noise in the scientific world.
CHEVRIER. Noise? What do you mean?
PIERRE. Well, the substance is susceptible to discharging a great deal of energy.

(PIERRE is starting to feel a little tipsy. He is trying to do everything in his power not to show it.)

CHEVRIER. A new source of energy. Interesting. *(PIERRE nods his head vigorously.)* But which one? Tell me more. *(PIERRE suddenly goes blank. He closes his eyes, his head falls forward, he squinches his eyebrows and shakes his head. CHEVRIER smiles.)* I understand. I'm a little too impatient. *(PIERRE nods his head affirmatively.)* Incidentally, how are you managing to communicate with Mademoiselle Machinska? *(PIERRE starts to laugh hysterically.)* What's so funny?
PIERRE. *(Suppressing his laughter, he now speaks with a distinctive slur combined with occasional precise enunciation.)* It's very s-s-simple, M-monsieur Chhhevrier. How cann I be aware of what herrr work isss if we don't even speak the saaame languagge. You musst be asssking yourseeelf ....
PIERRE. Yes, how do you manage?
PIERRE. Well ... I am ggoingg tooo tell yyou ... I communin ... communisni ... communicate with her ... because I ssspeak Ppolishhh ....
CHEVRIER. You stupefy me, my dear Curie.
PIERRE. F-f-f-luently.

(And he starts to laugh again.)

CHEVRIER. You really impress me. Because me, with languages, I just ... would you do me a big favor and tell this young person that Poland is a great country. With great people. And that I deplore the occupation by the Russians.

PIERRE. *(Still slurring.)* Most assuredly. *(To MARIE, who is visibly worried about all this.)* Dzisiajjj wieczzoremm ppapuga zygfrrrydd usadzieee dwah razzy naaa operzee bez pplaceniaaa.

(MARIE bows, as if grateful for what CHEVRIER has told PIERRE to tell her.)

CHEVRIER. Tell her that, thanks to people like her ...

PIERRE. *(Translates.)* Valdivstok peopleisky blakaka ...

CHEVRIER. ... science will be able to make great strides ...

PIERRE. *(Translates.)* ... sieansky progresiansky aleapski stridsky ...

CHEVRIER. ... and will culminate very quickly into a new golden age ...

PIERRE. *(Translates.)* ... culminaska, en agjinaski goldilokski ...

CHEVRIER. ... where all scientists will live as a fraternity without borders or frontiers.

PIERRE. *(Translates.)* ... trikoff scienceniskis tolstoy amussaka polenta frontierski.

CHEVRIER. Thank you so very much, my dear Curie.

PIERRE. *(Translating.)* Goodenov Curieni Anna Karenena.

CHEVRIER. No, no, it's you that I am thanking.

PIERRE. Oh, s-s-sorry.

MARIE. *(In a mock serious tone.)* Wodko, stodyczy moja ty jestes nazdrowie, ile cie cenic trezeba ten tylko sie dowie kto przeplacie.

CHEVRIER. What did she say?

PIERRE. *(Still slurring.)* Sheee wishhes to thannk you verrrry much. But she cannnot heeelp butt notice that youuu are causing grrreat painnn by standing on myyy foot, which issss absolutely coorrect.

(CHEVRIER has been, for a number of moments now, standing on PIERRE's foot. CHEVRIER steps away.)

CHEVRIER. I'm so sorry.
PIERRE. Noo proooblemmm.
CHEVRIER. Well, I'm delighted that you and Mademoiselle Trukovska are getting along so well. I expect big things from the two of you. Big things. Au revoir. *(He starts towards the door but is distracted by the bust of Pasteur for a moment.)* Strange. Pasteur is looking to his left on these new busts. It must have something to do with the socialists and the radicals who are slowly taking over our country.

(He exits.
MARIE immediately runs to the bust of Pasteur and straightens the head.)

MARIE. I was never so afraid in all my life. You were wonderful.

(PIERRE is having trouble staying on his feet.)

PIERRE. Woonderful? I lllied to my supperiorr … jussst to cover up allll your bussiness with Beemont. I fibbed and lied through my teeth.

(MARIE starts to laugh, almost uncontrollably.)

MARIE. What did you call my goulash?
PIERRE. Ragout of Sulfite of Polandrata.
MARIE. *(Laughs even harder.)* And the dynamite?
PIERRE. *(Starting to laugh as well.)* Dynoslavomite of the fanaticite.
MARIE. That's perfect.

(She laughs even more.)

PIERRE. Yess, well, even if I ammm drunk as a baaat, it doesn't stop me from being verry, verrry maaaad at you.

MARIE. You know, you're very amusing.

(She approaches him and hugs him. She then pulls him toward her for a kiss. PIERRE melts in her arms and he suddenly collapses, holding on to her for dear life.
BÉMONT enters.
PIERRE immediately pulls himself away.)

PIERRE. *(Covering up.)* Yess, perrrmonganate of sssodium. Absolutely, mademoiselle Sklodowska. Permagonate of sssodium.

BÉMONT. I understand you've had another visit from Herr Chevrier.

PIERRE. Yess, and I promisse you're gonnna lovvve thisss ssstory.

(Stage goes dark.)

Scene 4

(The laboratory towards the end of the morning.
The bust, the goulash and the vodka have all disappeared. MARIE is presently working with a potentiometer while PIERRE is studying the various parts of his electrometer, which is now disassembled.
We hear the muffled sound of an explosion in the distance. The glass windows shake. They don't notice it. A moment later, MARIE seems to be agitated.)

MARIE. This is even stronger.

PIERRE. *(Busy with his work.)* Mmh?

MARIE. Pierre, these uranium salts are actually scorching the potentiometer.

PIERRE. What are you talking about?

MARIE. Without being connected to an electrical current, these uranium salts are actually emitting electricity. True, it's very weak but still. Come see.

(PIERRE goes to her.)

    PIERRE. But that's absolutely impossible.
    MARIE. See for yourself.

(PIERRE examines closely and listens.)

    PIERRE. Like an electric battery. It's very bewildering. Where did you get these salts?
    MARIE. From the armoire.
    PIERRE. Well, anyway, uranium has no magnetic properties whatsoever.
    MARIE. And yet, it's emitting electricity. That would explain everything.
    PIERRE. Marie, how could it emit electricity? One would have to have stocked it with electricity since it can't produce any of its own.

(BÉMONT enters, visibly worried.)

    BÉMONT. Quick! Quick! I'm in shit up to my neck.
    PIERRE. Gustave, come here … listen to this.
    BÉMONT. *(Displaying some proof sheets.)* Look at this. When I developed the photo plates they were completely ruined. Look at this rectangular spot in the middle of these photographs.
    PIERRE. *(Looks over the proof sheet.)* You accidentally overexposed them, that's all.
    BÉMONT. In which case they would be white. But these are perfectly clean except for the spot on top, in the exact same place. *(To MARIE.)* What did you do to them?
    MARIE. Nothing. When Chevrier showed up I hid them in the armoire under this box of uranium salts. And Pierre got them to you as soon as you decided to develop them elsewhere.
    BÉMONT. *(Grabbing the small box.)* This is the exact same shape as the spot. The box is what ruined everything.
    PIERRE. *(Fascinated.)* It's completely insane, Gustave. Some-

thing must have gone through it.

BÉMONT. You realize that I'm in a real quandary now.

PIERRE. All you have to do is tell your uncle ....

BÉMONT. My uncle, my uncle ... my clientèle happens to be a bunch of rogues who hang around the Moulin Rouge. Characters like Red Beak, Pock Mark .... Me, they call Mister Science. These people walk around with razors in their pockets. They warned me. They pay cash ... but any dirty tricks or if I'm the least bit late, they'll drop by the school. They have my name, my address. I'm done for.

PIERRE. Do they know about Marie?

BÉMONT. No.

PIERRE. Now, just calm down. I'll speak to them and I'll explain that a most unusual phenomenon has occurred ....

BÉMONT. You can't be serious. You know what Lautrec told me? "Be straight with them. They're the type of people who will kill your mother *and* your father."

(Suddenly there's a loud knock at the door. They all freeze. BÉMONT indicates to please not say a word and to let him hide in the closet. He opens the closet door. It's filled with stuff but he manages to squeeze in.
The front door opens and it is GEORGETTE.)

PIERRE. This is not a good time, Mademoiselle Georgette.

GEORGETTE. I'll only be a minute. *(She heads right for MARIE.)* What is that thing that people drink in your country?

MARIE. In my country?

GEORGETTE. You know, that thing that men get drunk on at your place.

MARIE. Ah, you mean vodka.

GEORGETTE. That's it, vodka. Don't buy any more. The police came around and warned everybody that there's a certain vodka that nobody should drink. I think it's called CHEVRIKAIA. It's poisoned. They're looking for a woman.

PIERRE. A woman? What kind of woman?

GEORGETTE. A maniac kind of woman. So far she's sent eighty people to the hospital.

PIERRE. *(Suddenly realizing something.)* Did you say maniac or ammoniac?

GEORGETTE. What's ammoniac?

PIERRE. A very toxic product. Well, thank you very much for warning us. And if you don't mind, we really have to get back to work.

GEORGETTE. *(Starting to leave — shaking her head.)* CHEVRIKAIA.

(And she exits. BÉMONT steps out of the closet.)

PIERRE. *(To MARIE.* Is it possible that you were foolish enough to fabricate your mixture in old ammoniac drums from this school?

BÉMONT. Well, don't people rinse out their receptacles before returning them? It's very dangerous.

PIERRE. *(Enraged.)* I swear I'm going to let you have it. I've been patient long enough with you.

(MARIE comes between them.)

MARIE. Stop it, Pierre. Calm yourself.

BÉMONT. *(To PIERRE.)* You don't think I'm in enough trouble as it is?

MARIE. Please stop yelling at each other like a couple of idiots. All we need now is for … *(CHEVRIER enters in tatters from head to toe, as if a tiger had ripped his entire outfit: his jacket, his pants, his top hat.)* … that bloated Chevrier to show up with his asinine comments.

CHEVRIER. There's been an attempt on President Carnot's life. Thirty meters from me a bust of Pasteur blew up. It's a catastrophe.

PIERRE. Oh, my God.

CHEVRIER. Carnot is safe … but the Minister of Education was wounded. Now Binèt is going to get all the glory. He's next in line for the job.

BÉMONT. How badly is he wounded?

CHEVRIER. With my luck? Bad enough.

MARIE. You're sure about the bust of Pasteur?

CHEVRIER. Sure and certain.

MARIE. Could it not have been Victor Hugo? They look a great deal alike.

CHEVRIER. I am as sure as I heard you call me "that bloated Chevrier with the asinine comments." You know, for a Polish student who just the other day couldn't speak the language, you certainly manage quite nicely. Well, the asinine comments are over. The game is over. I'm cutting all coal supplies. And in one week if you haven't given me something to crush Binèt ... you're out on the street, all of you. Understood? Monsieur and Madam Curie? Understood, Carrot-head?

BÉMONT. What did you just call me?

CHEVRIER. Carrot-head. Carrot-face. Carrot-top. Carrot-nitwit. Do you want me to give you a complete list of all your nicknames engraved in every single lavatory in school?

BÉMONT. *(Pulling his shirtsleeves up.)* Okay, you big lout ....

CHEVRIER. Out! Get out of here!

BÉMONT. I'm the one who's deciding to leave. Watch what I'm going to do with my work coat. *(He takes off his smock, rips it savagely and throws it at CHEVRIER.)* There, now you put it on. It's the perfect clown outfit for a would-be scientist.

CHEVRIER. *(Going towards BÉMONT.)* I'm going to break you in two.

BÉMONT. *(Grabs a chair.)* You miserable cow dung. Let me get by or I'll pulverize you.

(There's a moment of hesitation and then all of a sudden BÉMONT discards the chair, throws himself against the door and exits, slamming the door behind him.)

CHEVRIER. *(To PIERRE and MARIE.)* Alright, who's next?

PIERRE. Monsieur Chevrier, I have nothing but passion for my work. I'm entirely devoted to science and this school. However, due to the present circumstances, I must respectfully render my resignation.

CHEVRIER. Both of you?

MARIE. No! *(To PIERRE.)* No, Pierre, maybe in a week ... but not now. Not when we're so close.

PIERRE. I'm sorry but I've made up my mind.

MARIE. *(To PIERRE.)* No! *(To CHEVRIER.)* Don't listen to him. One week, that's all we need. One week. I swear to you that in one week my husband and I will give you enough material to have you swimming in awards.

PIERRE. And I'm telling you ....

MARIE. Be quiet! Well, Chevrier?

CHEVRIER. Very well. One week. And I mean *one* week!

(He exits.)

MARIE. *(To PIERRE.)* If you love me, you'll wait one week.

PIERRE. If I love you. Of course I love you. I married you.

MARIE. That was for convenience. My convenience.

PIERRE. That's what you think.

MARIE. One week.

PIERRE. One week to find what?

MARIE. Pierre, listen to me. The two of us can do "anything." Do you hear me? Anything! You have a superior mind and I'm a workhorse. In one week we will find something.

PIERRE. But what?

MARIE. Something. We will, Pierre. If we want it badly enough, we will!

PIERRE. How do you say in Polish, "in numbers there is strength."

MARIE. Solidarnosc!

(Stage goes to dark.)

Scene 5

(The laboratory — one week later.
The pendulum clock indicates two minutes earlier. PIERRE and MARIE, wearing their coats, finish straightening out the labora-tory. They have two leather pieces of luggage resting on the floor.

PIERRE is sweeping the floor, while MARIE cleans off the black-board. They then go to the table and start looking at a large map.)

PIERRE. You know, Marie, we could leave from Chartres and come back through Dijon. We'd have all the way to the Pyrénées to get our legs in shape.

MARIE. But if we bicycled east right away, it would be much faster. *(CHEVRIER enters holding his pocket watch.)* Then on to the Jura Mountains ... and then the Alps. It's more gradual that way. Whereas the Pyrénées, after Lourdes, it's straight up.

(PIERRE has been staring at CHEVRIER.)

CHEVRIER. So, you're going to beg for laboratory work in all the pharmacies of our Republic? *(PIERRE and MARIE stand frozen.)* Shall we wait for the exact moment or do we go directly to your results?

PIERRE. As you wish.

CHEVRIER. Very well then, I'll simply pick up your copies ....

(He starts toward table.)

PIERRE. You can stop your buffoonery now.

CHEVRIER. This isn't buffoonery. This is jubilation. I'm either going to reap the honors I so richly deserve or I will have the pleasure of ridding the university of two parasites. It's what you might call my lucky day. I take it we're waiting till the very last moment. You have exactly ten seconds. *(He stands there looking at his pocket watch for the full ten seconds, and then:)* Now, tell me everything. Does your quartz continue to jump all over the place? Or did it calm itself with the uranium?

PIERRE. It continues to jump all over the place.

CHEVRIER. *(Mocking.)* Ah, too bad. Tsk, tsk, tsk.

MARIE. It proves that uranium emits, in its natural state, not only electricity but x-rays as well.

PIERRE. And the flux is regular and constant.

MARIE. The same x-rays that Roentgen discovered.

CHEVRIER. Are you trying to tell me that uranium produces energy? You think I'm going to tell that to the Academy?

PIERRE. *(Taking a thick envelope from the desk drawer.)* Not tell. Reveal. Prove. Demonstrate. Uranium, all the uranium in the world, since time immemorial, emits x-rays. We just didn't notice it before. And it does so in quantities that are strictly proportional to its mass. Two grams of uranium produce twice as many x-rays as one gram. And it's invariable from Johannesburg to Lyon.

MARIE. And we propose to call this phenomenon *radio-activity.*

CHEVRIER. You are seriously trying to make me believe that?

PIERRE. Verify our calculations, our experiments, our deductions. You don't have to believe. Just observe.

CHEVRIER. *(Opens the envelope.)* You realize that one cannot at the same time run a school and be up on all the concepts which are perpetually evolving in modern physics. I think you're trying to trap me in a hoax so that I can make an incompetent public demonstration, right?

MARIE. Just submit our work to someone in whom you have confidence.

PIERRE. With the hopes, of course, that that someone doesn't steal your thunder at the presentation.

MARIE. In other words, if you were to memorize this by heart, you could walk in with a swagger, sticking your chest out presenting these conclusions all by yourself.

CHEVRIER. *(Putting down the notes.)* I'm reinstating your supply of coal. You lock yourselves in the lab, you explain everything to me from A to Z and, if I'm able to verify and understand everything … then I'll decide what I shall do next.

PIERRE. *(Putting away the notes.)* No, I'm afraid not. You see, we're leaving on our honeymoon.

MARIE. We bought ourselves some bicycles.

PIERRE. You told us one week, period. That was the understanding.

MARIE. Now, you have to tell us if we are fired or not.

PIERRE. If we are being sent away …

MARIE. We'll bring our research notes with us.

PIERRE. On our little tour de France ….

MARIE. Who knows? It might make quite an impression in, oh, let's say ... Zurich.

PIERRE. Where there seems to be a great deal of interest in x-rays.

MARIE. Imagine if the British had sent Newton away.

PIERRE. The shame.

MARIE. Well then, Chevrier, a decision.

CHEVRIER. I'm thinking.

MARIE. You had better think quickly because we're leaving in exactly ... thirty seconds. Which is twenty more than you gave us. *(To PIERRE.)* Did you remember to bring the air pump?

PIERRE. In the gray bag.

(MARIE goes to the bag and looks in and comes up with a small apparatus.)

MARIE. And what is this?

PIERRE. A gift for you. It's a small traveling version of my electrometer. It'll come in handy when we start camping outside near the end of April. I've noticed that the vibration attracts flies and as they pass between the electrodes, the electric arc seems to give them a coronary.

MARIE. You're fantastique. I too have a wedding gift for you.

(She hands him a book.)

PIERRE. *(Reading the title.)* "Periodic Classification of Atomic Masses as Expressed in Moles from Elements Identified by Mendeleieff." Nothing could make me happier.

(He goes toward MARIE. They embrace.)

CHEVRIER. Bingo! I'll do it. Pass me the newborn. I may be making a massive blunder. However, you two are just crackers enough to have found something by pure chance. Alright, I'm throwing myself into this up to my neck. But, be warned .... If you've taken advantage of me and if you've misled me, you can peddle all the way

to Madagascar but I'll still find you. And when I find you I'll squash
you, I'll reduce you to pulp. I'll ....

PIERRE. *(At the door with MARIE and their luggage.)* We shall
see what we shall see!

(They exit.
CHEVRIER remains there motionless for a moment, and then plunges
    into the notes. Takes out a photographic proof sheet and holds it
    up to the light. He starts to react ....)

Curtain

End of Act I

ACT II

Scene 1

(Four years later.
The laboratory is pretty much the way it was in ACT I, except that it has evolved. There's a rug now, a second armoire. Where there were only a couple of chairs, now there's a sofa. It is summer. Some of the windows are open. We can hear birds chirping in the distance.
PIERRE and MARIE are busy working. MARIE, without having become part of the haute couture, is nonetheless wearing a nice little summer dress that is very charming and suits her. PIERRE is in his shirtsleeves; his smock is open. He is showing a letter to MARIE.)

PIERRE. Look, the University of Baltimore is inviting us to come to a conference on radioactivity. We can choose whichever date we want. What shall I answer?

MARIE. I thought we were finished with the scientific circus. Tell them we don't go to conferences anymore and send them that speech we gave in London. Beside, we have nothing more to say regarding radioactivity. It's been months now.

PIERRE. But still, it's the United States. A country that is growing by leaps and bounds.

MARIE. If the international scientific community doesn't leave us alone, we're going to wind up falling behind others in the study of uranium x-rays. There's that English gentleman ....

PIERRE. Rutherford?

MARIE. Yes, Rutherford. I'm worried about him. He's moving at an incredible pace.

PIERRE. Look, we each pull our own weight. That's the way it is in the world of science.

MARIE. Well, it's not fair. After all, I was the first one in the world who had the intuition that uranium emitted x-rays. I'm the one who baptized the phenomenon "radioactivity." It's very frustrating to be the one who only opens the road.

PIERRE. I guess we won't be going to Baltimore.

(Through the windows, we suddenly see a pair of arms holding an old photo apparatus with magnesium flash. The flash goes off.)

MARIE. Stop that! Enough!

(PIERRE immediately runs out to apprehend the paparazzo. A moment later he reenters.)

PIERRE. He got away.

MARIE. How are we supposed to work under these conditions?

(There's a knock at the door.)

MARIE. Now what?

PIERRE. *(Dryly.)* Enter!

(It's BÉMONT, dressed like a prince, wearing kid gloves, a gray pearl bowler, spats, etc.)

BÉMONT. It's me. Gustave. Am I interrupting?

PIERRE. Gustave. Marie, it's Gustave.

MARIE. Gustave.

(They run towards him and embrace him affectionately.)

PIERRE. It's been forever.

BÉMONT. Four years.

MARIE. This is unbelievable. Four years without any news and this morning, I was just saying to Pierre, what could have happened to good old Gustave and his patents?

PIERRE. Obviously something good. Or you wouldn't be dressed like royalty.

BÉMONT. Business is brisk.

MARIE. And your research?

BÉMONT. I've realized my dream. I finance my own research. I have a lab in my backyard. I can now devote myself entirely to the spectroscopy. And what about the two of you? Tell me about all the commotion you've caused during these four years.

MARIE. You don't know the half of it. It's almost impossible to work quietly around here.

BÉMONT. I read in the *Scientific Academy Gazette,* thanks to you two, Chevrier finally got his laurels.

PIERRE. Ah, yes. Those famous laurels. The day the university honored him, he walked around the neighborhood bursting with pride. He had photos taken from every angle imaginable.

(There's a knock at the door. And without waiting for an answer, the door opens. It's GEORGETTE. She is now dressed in the style of the day, holding a rather ornate bassinet, covered by a net that is used to keep flies away.)

MARIE. And here is Mademoiselle Georgette.

(GEORGETTE seems very pleased to see BÉMONT and anxious to talk to him, but mimics that she doesn't want to wake up the baby.)

BÉMONT. *(Half whisper.)* Mademoiselle Georgette.

GEORGETTE. *(Half whisper.)* Monsieur Carrot-f ... uh, Bémont, I mean Bémont.

MARIE. *(Half whisper.)* And, this is little Irène.

BÉMONT. *(Going to the baby.)* Oh, let me see this angel. *(He follows GEORGETTE, who has gone to deposit the bassinet in a corner of the lab. BÉMONT looks through the net tenderly and then goes back and joins the Curies. To PIERRE.)* Well, she's a lucky one. At least she didn't wind up with your idiotic expression.

PIERRE. Go ahead and make fun. They tell me she is extremely advanced for her age.

GEORGETTE. Well, with parents like you, the very day she was born, you could tell she was already educated.

BÉMONT. So, then, Mademoiselle Georgette, you've given up the restaurant business?

GEORGETTE. I had the audacity to slap my boss for pinching my rear end. I was fired, like you.

MARIE. And ever since, Mademoiselle Georgette is paid by the university to take care of Irène.

GEORGETTE. If only I didn't have the baby carriage. Monsieur Curie made it. I don't think I'll ever get used to it.

PIERRE. *(To BÉMONT – proudly.)* I made the carriage out of bits and pieces of two of our old bicycles.

GEORGETTE. It's the talk of Parc Luxembourg.

BÉMONT. That bad, huh?

GEORGETTE. Let me show it to you.

(She exits.)

PIERRE. *(Shakes his head.)* Now, tell me, what else is going on?

BÉMONT. Oh, I almost forgot. I brought you a complete catalogue of everything that I've patented that is now on the market. You go ahead and choose anything you want.

(He takes out a catalogue and hands it to them.)

MARIE. That's very kind of you.

PIERRE. *(Looking through the catalogue.)* Let's see … hair clippers, bean sowers, neutering tongs ….

BÉMONT. Look more towards the back pages.

MARIE. You mean you go from laboratory to laboratory yourself?

BÉMONT. In a manner of speaking, when it's convenient. Go ahead, keep looking. Show me what will give you pleasure.

PIERRE. Why don't we look at it on our own, and tell you later.

BÉMONT. But of course.

(GEORGETTE reenters with the baby carriage. It is a mishmash of

wheels and bicycle parts — handlebars and lights that hang on the front and on the sides, as well as a bag that hangs to one side. It's quite a contraption.)

GEORGETTE. Here it is. The monstrosity.

BÉMONT. *(Looks it over.)* Yes, well, uh, I can see where it makes quite an impression.

PIERRE. You don't like it?

BÉMONT. I didn't say that but ....

MARIE. I find in cunningly crafted and it's certainly economical, but aesthetically speaking ....

GEORGETTE. Everybody stares at us in the parc. There's a whole group of nannies, and the minute I approach them, they run off in every which direction.

MARIE. You know, Pierre, maybe we should invest in something a little more ... decent.

PIERRE. But it costs a fortune. You know the expenses we have since Irène was born. *(To BÉMONT.)* Might you not have a pram in your catalogue?

BÉMONT. *(Inspects the baby carriage.)* No, but I think I have an idea. *(He quickly takes out a Swiss penknife and starts to dismantle the pram. He unscrews, he bends, he eliminates, he pulls apart, he redresses, he reassembles, and in doing so, leaves half of the pieces on the floor. The result is a rather elegant-looking pram and a much lighter one. Please note: during this operation, BÉMONT is heard to say things like "There, that does it;" "This is better;" "This should help;" "Now we've got something;" "Here we go," etc., etc., etc. Indicating the new pram, he continues.)* Well, what do you think?

MARIE. Magnifique.

GEORGETTE. Miraculous.

PIERRE. Well, I suppose it is a little more decent-looking, though definitely more banal.

GEORGETTE. *(As she wheels the pram back and forth.)* And look how it turns so much better. And for the sidewalks, it will be a lot easier.

(She then proceeds to push the pram full speed all over the lab, mak-

*ing sharp turns in the process. This suddenly causes baby IRÈNE,
in her bassinet, to start crying. PIERRE goes over and picks up
IRÈNE and puts her in the pram.)*

PIERRE. Well, time to go test the crowd at the Luxembourg.
GEORGETTE. *(As she leaves with the new, sleeker pram.)* Au
revoir, Monsieur Bémont. It was a pleasure seeing you and thank you
so much. *(To the baby.)* We're on our way. We're going to pretend we
don't even see those other nannies.

(She exits.)

MARIE. *(To BÉMONT.)* You might want to consider taking a
patent out on that as soon as possible.
BÉMONT. Believe me, innovation is only profitable if it corre-
sponds to demand. I finally understand that now. For instance, you
Pierre, with your Piezo electric quartz, had you had it patented … especially with your discovery of uranium, you would be making a fortune by now.
PIERRE. You would have us hold back our discovery for merce-
nary reasons? I can't believe you. What infamy!
BÉMONT. Look, I'm not here to argue. I say God bless all discoveries. But just a word in passing. If you've recently uncovered
methods to collect or channel or convert the energy that is emitted by
uranium, I want you to know that I'm very interested. I'm telling you
that just in case. Especially now that you have a family.
PIERRE. *(Coldly.)* Good. Duly noted.
BÉMONT. So then, where are you in your research?
PIERRE. Marie is marking time a bit and I've gone back to my
hobbies.
BÉMONT. *(Surprised; to MARIE.)* You're marking time?
MARIE. Well, one might say that.
BÉMONT. What exactly is radioactivity telling you these days?
MARIE. Many things but nothing that makes any sense.
BÉMONT. For example?
MARIE. Are you with Scotland Yard?
BÉMONT. I'm sorry but your research has always fascinated me.

Am I being too indiscreet?

PIERRE. You know Marie, to a scientist, curiosity is a cardinal virtue.

BÉMONT. *(Embraces the two of them warmly.)* No, Marie is right. It's premature. Go ahead, do your work. I'm leaving. I'll see you both soon. Bémont has resurfaced.

(During that last sentence, CHEVRIER has entered.)

CHEVRIER. So I noticed. *(BÉMONT turns, shows a little panic but CHEVRIER reassures him.)* Don't worry, Bémont, the past is forgotten. Surely you won't refuse to shake my hand.

(The shake hands.)

BÉMONT. Monsieur Le Directeur, it is obvious that your new stature in the scientific community has given you a certain … élan.

CHEVRIER. And prosperity seems to have conferred on you a certain … distinction. What exactly are you up to these days?

BÉMONT. Well, one of my activities consists of providing experimental materials to laboratories. I brought Marie and Pierre a catalogue which you are more than welcome to peruse. I'll be happy to give you twenty percent off.

CHEVRIER. That sounds wonderful, but I'm going to have to ask you to leave us. I must speak to my two friends here.

BÉMONT. May I get in touch with you in the future?

CHEVRIER. Excellent idea. Au revoir, Bémont.

BÉMONT. *(A little obsequious.)* Au revoir, Monsieur Chevrier. I'm honored. *(As he leaves, to PIERRE and MARIE.)* Au revoir, "friends."

(He exits.)

CHEVRIER. *(Taking out a magazine from his pocket.)* My children, I've just read something fascinating. It seems that a certain Rutherford has published, this morning, in the *Royal Scientific Magazine*, some twenty pages contesting *all* of your conclusions.

MARIE. Our conclusions on radioactivity?

CHEVRIER. It seems that uranium derived from pitchblend, a wretched rock that can only be found in Austria, does not correspond to the norms of radioactivity that you have defined.

MARIE. *(Grabbing the publication from him.)* That's impossible.

PIERRE. No matter what rock you extricate, uranium is still uranium.

MARIE. And its radioactivity is constant.

CHEVRIER. I agree, believe me. What we're going to do then is draft a communiqué formally denying this nonsense. Furthermore, for certain influential newspapers, I hold firsthand some rather spicy information regarding the private life of this Rutherford. Journalists will have a field day. His goose is cooked.

MARIE. Rodolphe, that's not right. Before reacting, why don't we examine this article and let's redo all the numbers in support of all these experiments?

PIERRE. Yes, let us keep this on a ... scientific level.

MARIE. In the meantime, mum's the word.

CHEVRIER. But you don't understand, this is turning into a scandal. The president of the Academy conveyed to me, this morning, his utter stupefaction. And those were his exact words.

PIERRE. Let them say what they want. We shall see who laughs last.

CHEVRIER. How fast do you think you can cook this stew?

MARIE. *(Looking over the article.)* I would say, at the latest, two months.

CHEVRIER. Two months! I'm afraid that will not do at all.

MARIE. Why not?

CHEVRIER. You see, in a moment of weakness, I allowed my confrères to propose me for the vacant seat at the Academy of Sciences.

MARIE. *(Shocked.)* You mean the Minister of Education died from that explosion?

CHEVRIER. No. He became entangled in a ménage à trois and the husband decided to get rid of the "trois." Anyway, if we're not cleared of all suspicion, vis-à-vis Rutherford, at the latest, in three weeks, we will never be elected.

MARIE. I'm afraid that "we" are the victims of bad timing. Maybe "we" should retract "our" candidacy. In two months, "we" will have a much better chance.

CHEVRIER. Don't you understand? An academician doesn't die every month.

PIERRE. Without wishing to sound too cynical, one has to realize that certain immortals have a much higher rate of mortality than others.

(He laughs mischievously.)

CHEVRIER. If you worked twice as fast, and if I were to help you, isn't there a possibility that in three weeks it would be done?

MARIE. *(Still leafing through the magazine.)* That would be miraculous. Rutherford has gone pretty far with his experimentation.

CHEVRIER. Very well then. But I want you to know, this is not the way I planned it. If I remove my candidacy, I'm going to appear to have certain misgivings.

PIERRE. You? Misgivings? Never!

CHEVRIER. Binèt will wind up Minister of Education, where he will be able to flaunt his new position to his heart's content. He's three years younger than I am, you know. *(CHEVRIER takes a small pad from his pocket.)* Go ahead, order. Order anything you need. You have carte blanche. But please try to work miracles. Three weeks! That would give me enough time to reconsider.

MARIE. I promise you nothing.

CHEVRIER. I only ask you to try. *(He gets the coal bin.)* More coal!

(He exits, leaving his small pad on the table.
The stage goes dark.)

Scene 2

(Several days later.
It appears to be very hot out. PIERRE is in his shirt. MARIE has her
hair up. She seems very annoyed by the electrometer. At her feet
is a sack of ore with a German inscription on it.)

MARIE. Ah. Kourrva!

PIERRE. What's the matter?

MARIE. There's a problem with the pitchblend. The radiation is
not homogeneous. And it's too strong. Rutherford was right.

PIERRE. At least this time, they won't blame it on my apparatus.

MARIE. That's why I'm asking myself the question. Rutherford
effectuated all these measurements with a replica of your electrometer. It says so in the article.

PIERRE. Have you noticed, every time something goes wrong,
someone always blames my electrometer?

MARIE. *(Strongly.)* But, Pierre, uranium is uranium!

PIERRE. No point in screaming. It's not my fault.

(GEORGETTE enters holding baby IRÈNE.)

GEORGETTE. Phew, is it hot! What crowds in the parc today.
And thanks to our new pram, not a single person stared at us....
You'd think we didn't exist.

PIERRE. Was Irène a good girl?

GEORGETTE. Mostly. Tell me, Madame Curie, for tonight's
supper, what should we have?

MARIE. *(Distracted.)* Whatever you wish.

GEORGETTE. How about some chicken?

MARIE. Perfect.

GEORGETTE. Or a roast pork? It's been a while.

MARIE. *(A little annoyed.)* Whatever.

GEORGETTE. Oh, I almost forgot. You know the Beaulieus who
live above us? The one whose wife has a lover in the military? Well,
according to the concièrge ....

MARIE. Listen carefully, Georgette. I've told you this a hundred times. I detest malicious gossip.

GEORGETTE. By the way, my sister sent me her recipe for her puff pastry.

MARIE. *(Dryly.)* I don't give a damn.

GEORGETTE. That's because you don't know my sister's puff pastry.

MARIE. That mouth! Are you ever going to shut it?

GEORGETTE. *(Offended.)* Very well. I just came by to talk for a few moments, but if this is what you wish, I just won't speak to anyone anymore. And at home, I'll just stay in my room ....

MARIE. *(Feeling sorry.)* Can't you see I'm on edge these days. I have problems you cannot begin to imagine.

GEORGETTE. All you have to do is confide in me.

MARIE. These are very complicated problems. Believe me, you wouldn't be able to help.

GEORGETTE. Because I'm not educated?

PIERRE. Marie ....

MARIE. Very well, why not? *(She gathers her strength and continues.)* I'm going to simplify this. *(Showing her some powder in a receptacle.)* This is uranium. A metal like lead or iron that comes deep from within the mines. We've known uranium for over a century. However, Monsieur Curie and I have noticed, for some time now, that uranium is not a metal like others. Uranium, believe it or not, emits electricity. *(GEORGETTE immediately steps back.)* Wait, it gets better. It also emits rays that can actually penetrate cardboard, a wooden plank, even a mattress.

GEORGETTE. But how can that be?

MARIE. We don't know. Nobody in this world right now knows why or how. Monsieur Curie and I have merely observed that it functions at a distance, in an invisible fashion.

(She demonstrates with a fluttering hand movement.)

GEORGETTE. Like the radio?

MARIE. Exactly. Like the radio. As a matter of fact, I call this phenomenon radioactivity. Do you follow?

GEORGETTE. Of course. And that's what's causing you all these problems.

MARIE. Yes, well …. You see, whatever is not a living thing is a form of precise activity. For instance, a volcano, a cloud, water that's boiling, a log that's burning … either it's physics or it's chemistry.

GEORGETTE. Oh, I see. A potato that's boiling …?

MARIE. That's a phenomenon of physics. If you remove the potato and turn off the fire, the phenomenon stops. However, if you plunge a piece of chalk into some vinegar, unfortunately I don't have any ….

GEORGETTE. I do. In my bag.

MARIE. Let me see. *(GEORGETTE takes a bottle of vinegar, gives it to MARIE, who uncorks it and fills a test tube with it. She then puts a piece of chalk into it. It immediately starts to boil.)* There, you see? It's boiling. But without inducing any heat. Now, if you remove the chalk, it will continue to boil as long as there's still vinegar and some chalk. It's called chemistry. Acetic acid plus carbonate of calcium equals salt.

GEORGETTE. The devil you say.

MARIE. So then, with radioactivity, the question was to find out if it was a phenomenon of physics or chemistry. Well, do you know what? It's physics. Whether one wets it or mixes it with anything else. Whether one heats it or cools it off, uranium continues to "jump around," as Monsieur Chevrier says. That is to say, it continues to radiate. Without diminishing and without interruption. The more uranium in a mixture, the more the mixture is radioactive. That's all that changes.

GEORGETTE. I believe you.

MARIE. You're not the only one. I figured it out, I verified it, I demonstrated it, I published it. Now the whole scientific world has taken notice. *(Becoming more agitated.)* But now, I have this rock that comes from Austria called pitchblend … *(She goes to the blackboard and begins sketching. [See drawing A on page 80.] Still agitated.)* … which contains a little bit or uranium and a lot of stones, like so. *(She continues her sketching. [See drawing B on page 80.] Still agitated.)* … and which, at equal weight, is more radioactive than pure uranium. Which, of course, is not possible. A mixture of rock and uranium cannot be more radioactive than pure uranium. This is not chemistry.

GEORGETTE. Maybe it's something else that you haven't discovered.

MARIE. Something else? What do you mean, something else?

GEORGETTE. Well, something that you will no doubt discover. Maybe in the blendpitch. I mean, after all, with your education ….

MARIE. But we know what's in the stones. Bismuth, carnotite, some impurities. And neither bismuth nor carnotite is radioactive.

(She continues her drawing. [See drawing C on page 80.])

GEORGETTE. Well, maybe it's the impurities that are jumping all over the place.

MARIE. But those impurities don't even contain any metal. How do you expect them to be radioactive?

PIERRE. *(Suddenly alerted.)* You verified?

MARIE. No, but … if there are impurities, they would be infinitesimal. If there was metal amongst the impurities, it would have to be a thousand ... a million times more radioactive than the uranium in order to render the mixture more radioactive than pure uranium. *(There is a long moment as PIERRE and MARIE look at one another intensely.)* You … think maybe …?

PIERRE. We can easily verify it. We have all kinds of residue from which you've extracted the uranium. If, at equal weight, this residue is more radioactive than the uranium, that will be proof. *(He goes to the electrometer, after having weighed two equal quantities of residue and uranium.)* Look at this dial, Georgette. First the uranium. The needle shows 75. Now the residue. *(Excitedly.)* The needle is over 100. This is unbelievable!

MARIE. *(Equally excited.)* This is fantastique! So this metal, this residue, is so radioactive that we'll have to call it ... radioactum.

PIERRE. Radionum.

MARIE. Radium!

PIERRE. That's it. Radium!

(There's a moment of emotion as PIERRE and MARIE look at each

other.)

GEORGETTE. *(Finally.)* Well, then, if you no longer need my help ….

(She heads for the door and exits.)

MARIE. In order to counter Rutherford, it won't suffice just to detect the radium. If we really want to present a decisive demonstration, we're going to have to extract it. Let's say it's diluted at one in a hundred thousandths, how much pitchblend are we going to need to produce one gram?

PIERRE. If my arithmetic is correct, I'd say one ton.

MARIE. *(Reaching for the order book that CHEVRIER left behind.)* We'll order two, just to be safe.

(Stage goes dark.)

Scene 3

(Several days later, the blackboard has now been pushed in a corner, as well as much of the material. What indicates that time has passed are two piles of sacks. The empty ones, which are numerous, have been carefully piled up to one side. The full ones, which number six or seven, are lying near the front door.

The stage right table is covered with containers that are placed in order of descending height, from a large kettle to a small test tube. The containers hold pitchblend at the different stages of refinery.

PIERRE and MARIE are covered with dust from the pitchblend and appear to be exhausted. MARIE is wearing a small shawl over her head. She's blending the mineral in a large kettle, with the aid of a steel bar. PIERRE empties the last remnants of a sack then puts it on top of the others. He holds his lower back as if it's hurting him. He then comes over and watches the pitchblend as it's being refined into the very last test tube.)

PIERRE. This bismuth is very discouraging. I've tried everything. I've fed it the most appetizing, alluring molecules imaginable and it's still marble.

MARIE. Eventually it will crack.

PIERRE. Let me take over.

(PIERRE replaces her at the kettle. MARIE goes to a corner of the table and sits ajar for a few moments.)

MARIE. How much have we done so far?

PIERRE. We're approaching the one ton mark. I know because the pile outside seems to have been cut by almost half.

MARIE. That's all?

PIERRE. You're not discouraged, are you?

MARIE. Not at all. But it does remind me of our climb through the Pyrénées. I'm anxious to reach the summit.

PIERRE. Unfortunately, the summit is not measured by tons of pitchblend but rather by milligrams of radium. Think of it as our first day in Chartres.

MARIE. That's encouraging.

(CHEVRIER enters.)

CHEVRIER. What a mess! The place looks like a shipyard. So, how are my geniuses?

PIERRE. *(Giving him a slight nod.)* Professeur.

(MARIE simply nods without speaking.)

CHEVRIER. The situation is somewhat delicate. From the four corners of the globe, it seems that the French scientific community is being bombarded with questions, more or less courteous, regarding what seems to be developing into an affair of state. If radioactivity, as Rutherford seems to suggest, is nothing more than a disengagement of energy caused by a slow chemical reaction between uranium and the rock which contains it, the world is going to cry "imposters." I would like you to assure me that this is not the case.

PIERRE. *(Indicating the entire laboratory.)* We're working on it.

CHEVRIER. I find it hard to believe that all this pitchblend is needed to extract uranium?

(PIERRE is about to say something.)

MARIE. Monsieur Chevrier, a little patience.

CHEVRIER. Patience? If you don't tell me how to answer all those questions, what are we going to look like?

PIERRE. Silent scientists. All you have to do is tell them that we're working.

CHEVRIER. *(As he looks around the room.)* What are you trying to prove with all this? You can, at least, tell *me*.

PIERRE. I'm sorry. Not you, not anyone.

CHEVRIER. But I'm your superior in this hierarchy.

MARIE. Maybe. But when it comes to molecular physics, it's all Greek to you. All you're doing is making us waste time. We asked you to wait, to be patient, so please be patient and wait!

CHEVRIER. *(Insulted.)* What do you mean, all Greek to me?

MARIE. Admit it. You don't know a crock about what we're doing.

CHEVRIER. *(Becoming more agitated.)* I just want you to understand that I was not given this position at the Sorbonne because I had an encyclopedic knowledge of all disciplines, but to help make France the boutique of experimental sciences.

MARIE. Who's stopping you?

CHEVRIER. You are! In refusing to give me proper information. *(Banging his fist on the table.)* Son-of-a-bitch, bastard, goddamn you! Are you or are you not going to tell me what you're doing with all this crap!

MARIE. *(Calmly.)* I'm sorry, but no.

PIERRE. It's premature. Please be patient.

CHEVRIER. Be patient? I just received the statement from Austria. Do you know what those two tons of pitchblend cost? Three thousand francs. Plus two thousand francs for transportation. That's two years' salary for a workman. You're going to bankrupt the school.

PIERRE. Rodolphe, we are about to make a decisive discovery.

MARIE. Which will have you elected directly into the Academy. Patience.

CHEVRIER. Cheats! Bandits! Swindlers! You managed to get away with a pseudo discovery four years ago. I'm afraid that today the luster is vanishing. You pose as martyred excavators of science, to give an illusion, but it doesn't work anymore. Everyone is becoming conscious of the absurdity of all this flash-in-the-pan. Two *tons* of flash-in-the-pan, one might say. You're imposters!

MARIE. I will not permit you to speak that way.

CHEVRIER. I'm giving you exactly two weeks to publish a paper. At which time, I disavow you publicly. And you're lucky this is the summer or else I'd be cutting off your coal supply.

(He exits in a rage. PIERRE and MARIE quietly continue to work. After a while, GEORGETTE enters. She seems to be pouting.)

GEORGETTE. I need to talk to you.

PIERRE. Later, Georgette, later.

GEORGETTE. No, now. Because what I have to say is not easy.

PIERRE. Alright, but quickly.

GEORGETTE. I'm handing in my resignation.

PIERRE. What?

MARIE. But why?

GEORGETTE. I've had another offer. From the Beaulieus. They're very decent people.

MARIE. You mean, not like us.

GEORGETTE. Well, they're people who have a family life and they see their children. They don't come home every day covered with soot. They're not indebted to all the merchants in town.

MARIE. Very well, Georgette. I'm just going to ask you to take Irène to my sister and tell her what you just told us. After which, you can run off to the Beaulieus. Au revoir and thank you for everything.

PIERRE. Au revoir, Georgette.

GEORGETTE. Well, I must say, you're taking it rather well. It just goes to show, I'm nothing but dung around here. We work like slaves for our bosses and they don't give a fig. Well, I'm going to tell you something. It's you who are dung. To study like this, to wind up drudging like ordinary workmen who don't even have respect for workmen. I call that double dung.

(She exits, slamming the door behind her. PIERRE and MARIE continue to work. The door opens once more. This time, it's BÉMONT.)

BÉMONT. What have you done to Mademoiselle Georgette? We came face to face and then she threw me against the building.

MARIE. We are not suitable enough. We have debts.

PIERRE. We are dung.

BÉMONT. Well, the truth is, when one sees you like this ....

PIERRE. Yes? So?

BÉMONT. I can't imagine what you're looking for, pounding away at rocks like a couple of galley slaves. You have to admit, you do look pitiful

PIERRE. You think this is amusing to us? You think we don't have a good reason for doing this?

BÉMONT. Oh, I don't doubt it. And at the risk of repeating myself, you could at least have hired some help. If you had entrusted me with a ....

PIERRE. Yes, I know. A patent. Frankly, I'm sick of your patents. I believe that science must remain pure. Pure, do you hear? Because, if truth be known, commerce has sucked you up. It has swallowed you, engulfed you. Your objective was to finance your own researches. What have you researched in the last four years, besides money? Nothing! Nothing from nothing!

BÉMONT. Guilty.

PIERRE. Four years shot to hell ... for money. Believe me, there are metals that are more interesting.

BÉMONT. You know, it's easy to make fun of money when you're the son of a doctor and you've always lived in the lap of luxury.

PIERRE. Me? In the lap of luxury?

BÉMONT. Well, more than me. I'm the son of a grocer. My family had to sacrifice themselves for me. So now I have to give the appearance of opulence. My mother had to work outside in the cold, with swollen hands and arthritis, so that she could one day see me wearing spats. So, I wear spats. Once a week, I take them to a café and we drink absinthe. And we listen to a fat tenor sing songs about workers in the fields. And you know what? I love it. It makes me happy. So I'm going to let a pathetic figure like you teach me a lesson?

PIERRE. Out! Get out of here! Your arthritis, your absinthe, your spats and your tenor. And you know what you can do with all of them.

BÉMONT. Never mind.

(He exits, slamming the door shut.
Time passes. MARIE goes back to her kettle. Suddenly she freezes and seems to be tottering, as if overcome with some sort of illness. PIERRE rushes to her. He goes to hold her but she has already sat down. She gently but firmly pushes him away.)

PIERRE. Marie, what is it?

MARIE. Nothing. It's probably the heat. I'm feeling better now. It's passing.

PIERRE. You're exhausted. I'm completely irresponsible to let you slave away like this.

MARIE. It's passed, I tell you.

PIERRE. I'm going to take you back to the house.

MARIE. It's over. I'm fine.

PIERRE. I don't want you to work here anymore.

MARIE. What?!

PIERRE. I'm going to finish refining this myself. This isn't work for a woman. You can come back for the final phase.

MARIE. You're not serious.

PIERRE. I'm absolutely serious.

MARIE. You have no right.

PIERRE. I don't have the right to stop my wife from ruining her health?

MARIE. Exactly. You have no right.

PIERRE. But why? Why break your back doing work that requires no scientific talent whatsoever, while we let our daughter live with your sister?

MARIE. Because I love it. This is where I'm happy.

PIERRE. You're happy here?

MARIE. Yes. Like a mad woman. Because here, in these containers, is a supernatural, unknown metal which is going to explode in the world of science. And I have the opportunity to be partners in its discovery. Me, a woman. Me, a Polack. I never dreamed of such glory when I was taking care of sniveling children to pay for my studies. And you want me to go wipe Irène's derrière because of a little dizziness? Tell me, Pierre, who do you think you married, anyway?

PIERRE. A great soul, a brilliant mind, and a sensational scientist.

MARIE. How about some moral qualities?

PIERRE. Of course. Self-denial, abnegation, dedication, and, of course, self-sacrifice.

MARIE. Ah, that's where the misunderstanding lies. You see me as some sort of Joan of Arc of the science community.

PIERRE. Well, even though you're making light of it, that image is not exactly false.

MARIE. *(With total honesty.)* The image *is* false. I do not believe in sacrifice or in dedication. It's amazing to me that one can live with someone and not even know that person. I believe in pleasure, Pierre. Uniquely in pleasure. The pleasure of looking, of searching, of finding, of understanding. The pleasure of beating our competitors to the punch. The pleasure of science, Pierre. For me, it's totally physical. It's like a drug. Far from having the feeling that I'm sacrificing myself, I have the feeling of sacrificing everything to that drug. Do you see the nuance there?

PIERRE. If I do understand correctly, you consider yourself a monomaniacal egocentric with certain perverse tendencies.

MARIE. Precisely!

(The two of them smile affectionately at one another.)

PIERRE. Whose vice it is to stick her nose into the secrets of matter.

MARIE. Exactly.

PIERRE. Well, then, what are we waiting for? Let's stir up that pitchblend until we have the pleasure of dropping.

(He opens his arms. She hugs him, snuggles up to him.)

MARIE. Please don't send me back to our flat.

(A moment while the two of them stay embracing each other. Suddenly MARIE jumps back.)

PIERRE. What is it?
MARIE. To separate the radium from the bismuth, we haven't tried any gas.
PIERRE. True. What are you thinking of?
MARIE. Hydrogen sulfite.
PIERRE. Hydrogen sulfite? *(He thinks for a moment.)* My God … that's an idea.

(He gets a bottle of gas, turns it upside down onto a metal support. He pours some powder into a glass jar that he then screws into the support, upside down. He opens the decompressor. A chemical reaction materializes in the glass jar. A mist appears and then dissipates. The inner sides of the glass jar remain grayish.)

MARIE. There was a reaction.

(PIERRE opens the glass jar, rubs a piece of cotton on the face of it and proceeds to analyze it at the electrometer.)

PIERRE. *(Excitedly.)* The needle is at the maximum. It shot to the very top. It's pure radium!
MARIE. We found it!

(The two of them sing and dance for joy in a wild, frenetic fashion, then finally regain their senses.)

PIERRE. *(Indicating the sacks of pitchblend.)* All we have to do now is crush, dissolve, filter, gather and crystallize a thousand more of these and then we'll have it. There's no time to waste. Shall we resume?

MARIE. There is one thing more urgent.

(She runs to the door and locks it.)

PIERRE. What? *(MARIE starts unbuttoning her dress.)* Here?
MARIE. On the sacks.

*(PIERRE starts unbuttoning his shirt. He's having trouble as ...
Stage goes dark.)*

Scene 4

(The next morning.
It's almost seven in the morning. Everything has been cleaned up, piled neatly. The number of empty sacks has doubled. On top of this pile of sacks lies CHEVRIER. Two empty bottles of alcohol have rolled on the floor nearby.
PIERRE and MARIE enter, a little exhausted but ready to work. He trips.)

PIERRE. You didn't lock up last night after we left?
MARIE. I would have sworn I did.
PIERRE. What about the armoire?
MARIE. Oh, my God, quick. Let's look.

(They both run to the armoire. PIERRE takes out a key, turns it three times and opens the door. Then he pulls out a small metal box which he deposits on the table. He proceeds to unlock the padlock on the box, out of which he takes a smaller box that he also unlocks. In this smaller box, there's an even smaller one that has a combination lock, which he proceeds to open. He then removes a test tube containing some gray powder. The tube is sealed with

a cork.)

MARIE. *(Relieved.)* Thank God.

(PIERRE lets out a shriek as he notices CHEVRIER.)

PIERRE. Ahh!!!
MARIE. Chevrier!
PIERRE. What is he doing here?
MARIE. Do you think he's dead?

(PIERRE goes toward CHEVRIER and takes his hand.)

PIERRE. He's warm. Chevrier! Chevrier! Rodolphe!

(There is no reaction.)

MARIE. Is he breathing?

(PIERRE gets closer to CHEVRIER.)

PIERRE. He reeks of cognac. *(He then notices the two bottles and indicates them to MARIE.)* He is dead drunk.

(He lifts one of CHEVRIER's eyelids. There's no reaction.)

MARIE. For him to be that drunk, something awful must have happened.
PIERRE. It's the pressure.
MARIE. How bad is his pressure.
PIERRE. No, I mean the international scientific pressure. He's carrying all of that on his shoulders. It's too much tension.
MARIE. Well, let's wake him up.

(They clap their hands, they make him smell all kinds of mixtures. Nothing is working.
There's a knock at the door. They immediately cover CHEVRIER with

some sacks and quickly hide the valued test tube.)

PIERRE. Come in.

(BÉMONT enters with a suitcase under his arm.)

BÉMONT. It's me again.
PIERRE. Gustave, don't take this wrong but you cannot come by here after what we've said to one another. It's too upsetting.
BÉMONT. Mea culpa. I have come to ask forgiveness. You opened my eyes. I sold all my patents. I locked myself in my lab and I said I wouldn't come out until I gave birth to this.

(He indicates the suitcase.)

PIERRE. What is it?
BÉMONT. The Bémont spectroscope. The first apparatus in the world to not only detect but also photograph spectral rays of everything that exists.
PIERRE. You can't be serious.
BÉMONT. *(As he pulls out a few photo prints.)* Here, look. Do you recognize iron? Nickel? Sulfur?
MARIE. This is wonderful.
BÉMONT. And you know what. Yesterday I obtained a patent and specifically told them I was making it part of public domain.
PIERRE. *You* did that?
BÉMONT. *I* did that.
MARIE. Are you feeling well?
BÉMONT. For the first time in my life. *(He smiles.)* Would you like a demonstration?
PIERRE. With pleasure.

(BÉMONT takes his suitcase and places it on a table. He opens it and produces an apparatus. He hands them a couple of glass slides.)

BÉMONT. Here. Put anything you wish onto these slides and I'll tell you exactly what it is just by looking through my spectroscope.

(While PIERRE and MARIE prepare some slides, BÉMONT polishes his spectroscope. When everything is ready, he plugs the apparatus into an electrical outlet. He looks into the viewfinder and then puts out a hand towards PIERRE and MARIE.) Let us begin. *(PIERRE and MARIE hand BÉMONT one slide at a time. BÉMONT looks at the results, one after another. After a second or two:)* Phosphorus ... fluorine ... beryllium ....

MARIE. This is very exciting.

BÉMONT. I'm telling you, *everything* that exists. Alright, what else? Next!

PIERRE. Just a moment.

(MARIE and PIERRE look at one another knowingly. They get the test tube. Opening it with tremendous precaution, they place a tiny portion of it onto a slide, then PIERRE hands it to BÉMONT.)

BÉMONT. *(His eyes glued to the apparatus.)* And this, uh, let me see. This ... it's not gold.... Uh, no, uh, let's see, it's not platinum. It's .... Oh, my God. My apparatus has gone haywire.

PIERRE. Can I see? *(BÉMONT, discouraged, lets them look while he verifies his apparatus. PIERRE continues, as he looks through the spectroscope.)* You don't know this one. It's radium.

BÉMONT. What?

MARIE. Radium

PIERRE. A new metal. That's what we've been searching for.

MARIE. Three hundred times more radioactive than uranium.

PIERRE. Atomic weight, two hundred and eleven point eighty-six.

MARIE. *(Showing BÉMONT the test tube.)* In here is a little more than a gram.

BÉMONT. You josh.

PIERRE. Do we look like joshers?

(After a moment or two, BÉMONT, still flabbergasted, examines the test tube and reflects. He becomes more and more confused and marveled by it.)

BÉMONT. May I ... may I photograph it?

MARIE. Be our guest.

BÉMONT. *(Getting ready to photograph.)* They found a new metal. Nothing less. These two idiots have discovered a new metal even dumber than uranium. Here, in this hovel that smells of old shoes. Okay, little radium, a big smile for Bémont. *(He presses the button. Loud noise and then silence.)* All we have to do now is develop this plate. *(To MARIE.)* Are you still equipped?

MARIE. Give.

(MARIE goes to the armoire and takes out her photographic equipment. She immediately starts working at it. After several moments, GEORGETTE enters. A little humbled but yet resolute.)

GEORGETTE. If I told you that I was coming back to take care of Irène, would you kick me in the rear or take me back?

PIERRE. But … what about the Beaulieus?

GEORGETTE. Don't even mention them to me. And those brats. To dress them, everything had to be just right. A half a day off a week. I had to eat in my own room. Look what I had to wear on my head. *(She pulls out a hat trimmed with ribbons and lace.)* I looked like a Cossack. And on top of that, no wine. Madame Beaulieu actually slapped me because I was smoking while I was walking the children. So I slapped her back. I never want to hear about them again. *(A beat.)* So? Are you taking me back?

PIERRE. *(To MARIE.)* Are we taking her back?

MARIE. To be truthful, Irène has been insupportable since you left. She's driving my sister crazy.

GEORGETTE. I'm not surprised. I mean ….

(BÉMONT goes and sits on the sacks where CHEVRIER is buried.)

BÉMONT. Have you told Chevrier about the radium?

PIERRE. Not yet.

BÉMONT. What are you waiting for?

PIERRE. We are waiting for him to resurface.

BÉMONT. Why? Where is he?

PIERRE. You're sitting on him.

(BÉMONT immediately jumps up and starts looking through the sacks and discovers CHEVRIER.)

BÉMONT. What is he doing there?

PIERRE. Apparently, he got drunk last night and fell asleep.

BÉMONT. Well, we have to wake him up.

PIERRE. Let him sleep it off. We tried everything. I'd rather you helped me carry him to his office.

GEORGETTE. Do you want me to go get the baby carriage?

BÉMONT. Wait. I want to put away my material and you, your radium.

(BÉMONT starts putting his material away. He unplugs the electric current from the end that is plugged into the apparatus, leaving the other still plugged into the wall. He lets fly the electric wire, which winds up on CHEVRIER, who immediately finds himself being electrocuted. CHEVRIER starts to bounce around like a madman. BÉMONT hurls himself towards the wall plug and pulls it out.)

CHEVRIER. *(Still having spasms .)* You're making a big mistake. You just executed an innocent man. I am not Captain Dreyfus. Stop firing!

BÉMONT. Chevrier! Chevrier! It's me, Bémont.

CHEVRIER. What are you doing at my place?

BÉMONT. We're at the university. In the laboratory of the Curies.

CHEVRIER. Oh, my head. What happened?

PIERRE. I think maybe you drank a little too much.

CHEVRIER. Oh, my God. Binèt.

PIERRE. Your friend Binèt? What about him?

CHEVRIER. He's dead.

PIERRE. When?

CHEVRIER. Last night.

MARIE. Where?

CHEVRIER. In my arms.

MARIE. What do you mean?

CHEVRIER. Coming out of the restaurant. There was nothing we could do. He suddenly had a seizure, he fell on the sidewalk and choked. Right there.

BÉMONT. You mean he saw himself die?

CHEVRIER. What horrible convulsions! *(He shudders.)* Brrr!

MARIE. Did he have children?

CHEVRIER. Four.

MARIE. Can you imagine anything worse?

CHEVRIER. Well, yes. It could have been me. I'm three years older. We have the same physique, we do the same work. I can't believe it. Had I been tempted like he was to have the kidney pie, I might also be dead. I had the veal. Just a lucky break.

BÉMONT. My poor Chevrier. However, I think we have something to pull you out of your depression. The Curies here have just made a great discovery. A new metal. Radium. Imagine, there's one more metal now.

CHEVRIER. One metal more, one metal less ....

BÉMONT. And you're the one who's going to present it to the Academy.

PIERRE. Yes, before the next election.

CHEVRIER. To be elected to Binèt's seat and to wind up like him two months later? In the middle of Boulevard Haussmann? Drowning in a sea of kidneys?

PIERRE. But surely, Rodolphe, you have to realize the importance of this discovery.

CHEVRIER. Last night, after he died, I wandered through the streets. I got drunk. Then I came here like a wounded rat. For after all, we're all rats. Laboratory rats. We run after prizes and laurels like rats in a labyrinth looking for cheese. And then one day, Boom! Drowned in kidneys. So, as far as the Academy is concerned, I don't give a fart. I want to sleep. I just want to be left alone to sleep. I'm just an old, tired rat. I'm weary. I'm an old, weary rat ....

(He falls over on the sacks.)

PIERRE. I would have expected anything but that.

MARIE. What if you gave him another shot of something?

BÉMONT. Too dangerous. If he pees in his pants, we might get an electric shock.

MARIE. But who's going to present our work to the Academy?

BÉMONT. Go and see Laroquette, Binèt's assistant.

PIERRE. What if Chevrier recovers and Laroquette is the one who gets elected to the Academy. He'll never forgive us.

MARIE. We could give him twenty-four hours.

GEORGETTE. What for? In war, if the leaders fall asleep, the soldiers have the right to walk all over them.

PIERRE. Yes, but all the same ... I mean ....

GEORGETTE. You know, for geniuses, you're really quite dumb. All this for a big oaf who only thinks of stuffing himself. A loudmouth who deprives you of coal? Who, I once heard call Monsieur Bémont "the little twit."

BÉMONT. He said that, "the little twit"?

GEORGETTE. I would double-cross him in a minute. I would take your invention and place it right in Laroquette's lap. Then I would let him take Chevrier's place and go in front of those old fuddy duddies. And the day that Laroquette was elected, do you know what I would tell Chevrier? I would tell him to ....

CHEVRIER. *(Suddenly, as a giant stepping out of the ocean.)* Shut up! Is the servant ever going to shut up? She's the only one you can hear around here! *(Slowly regaining his old self again.)* Enough babbling! Here is the plan. You give me a brief demonstration, I sign the communiqué and I let you lead the parade. The Academy is meeting today. We go there with vigor and determination. I jump up to the podium. I interrupt whatever debate is going on. I announce some burning new discovery and then I put the two of you in the spotlight and we watch ... *(Looks at GEORGETTE.)* ... the old fuddy duddies ... as their mouths drop and their teeth fall out. And after, we have a press conference. I'll rent the Hotel Crillon ....

GEORGETTE. *(To MARIE.)* It's just like with cows. When they don't want to get up, all you have to do is poke 'em in the belly with a hot iron, and pronto, they're standing at attention.

MARIE. *(As she takes a newly developed photo to CHEVRIER.)* And here is an x-ray photo of radium.

CHEVRIER. *(Opening his dossier.)* Drop it in the stew. Now let's go feed those old fogies.

(He walks toward the door.)

MARIE. *(To PIERRE.)* She's right. A little poke in the ribs, that's all it takes.

(She pokes him in the ribs.
Stage goes dark.)

Scene 5

(Later that evening.
We are once again in the laboratory. Moonlight is shining through the
*   windows.*
PIERRE and MARIE enter.)

MARIE. The electricity is still not working.

PIERRE. Be careful not to drop the radium. I think I drank a little too much champagne.

MARIE. Here, give it to me. Ooh, la, la. What a triumph! Were you watching the academicians?

PIERRE. And the journalists?

MARIE. Especially the English. Look … look what I see.

(As she starts to put away the radium they both suddenly notice it is
*   emitting a weak bluish glow.)*

PIERRE. *(Filled with wonder.)* Oh …!

MARIE. It's emitting light.

(She gets down on her knees.)

PIERRE. The light of the future, Marie. The light of the future.
(He joins her, facing her.)

MARIE. I feel like crying.

PIERRE. Because you foresee all the good, mankind will produce with this new energy?

MARIE. No. Because we're going to receive the Nobel Prize. *(Tearfully.)* And I have nothing to wear!

(The embrace warmly.)

(Final curtain.)

APPENDIX / MARIE'S DRAWINGS

Drawing A
(page 60)

Drawing B
(page 60)

Drawing C
(page 61)

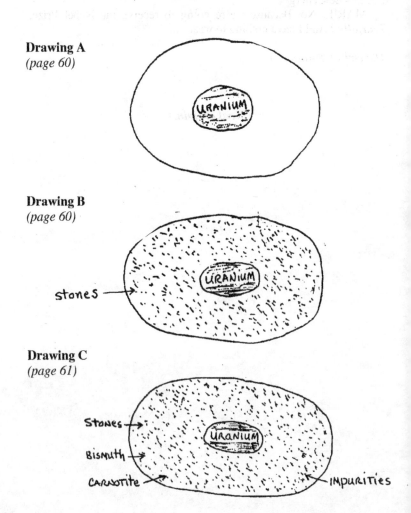

PROPERTY PLOT

ACT I – Scene 1

PRESET
Bucket of coal near stove
Coat rack with two smocks hanging
Photo plates and proof sheets
A musical contraption (Acoustophone) in armoire

PROP TABLE

PIERRE
Half-torn briefcase filled with papers and a pen

BÉMONT
A wooden chair with cushion that is easily breakable
A small bottle of cognac

CHEVRIER
Note paper

MARIE
A small pocket dictionary
Pencil
Eye glasses
Handbag containing photograph

ACT I – Scene 2

PRESET
Electrometer with electric plug on table
Bottle of ammonia
Rag
Crucible and demijohn on table

ACT I – Scene 3

PROP TABLE

BÉMONT
Heavy parcel containing the bust of Pasteur with head that screws on
and off

MARIE
Handbag with photograph in it
A two-handed basket containing a large cooking pot and a package of
powder

ACT I – Scene 4

Strike the goulash, Pasteur's bust and the vodka

PRESET
A potentiometer
A dissembled electrometer
Small box in armoire

PROP TABLE

BÉMONT
Photographic proof sheets

ACT I – Scene 5

PRESET
Two pieces of luggage
Broom
Large map
Thick envelope in desk drawer

PROP TABLE

CHEVRIER
Pocket watch

MARIE
A small electrometer in her bag
A small book, also in her bag

<u>ACT II – Scene 1</u>

PRESET
New rug
A second armoire
A sofa

EXTERIOR
Photo apparatus with magnesium flash

PROP TABLE

GEORGETTE
Bassinet
Baby carriage made of discarded bicycle parts

BÉMONT
Catalogue
Swiss pen knife

CHEVRIER
Magazine
Small writing pad

ACT II – Scene 2

PRESET
A sack of ore with German writing

PROP TABLE

GEORGETTE
Handbag with small bottle of vinegar in it

ACT II – Scene 3

PRESET
A pile of empty sacks
Another pile of 6 or 7 sacks
A series of containers wet on table starting with a large kettle all the
    way down to a small test tube
A steel bar (to stir)
A gas bottle
A piece of cotton

ACT II – Scene 4

PRESET
Two empty liquor bottles
Small metal box, in armoire, with small padlock
A smaller box within it, also with lock
An even smaller box in that one with combination lock
Small test tube with cork
A dossier (file) for Chevrier
Photographic equipment in armoire

PROP TABLE

BÉMONT
Suitcase containing a spectroscope with viewfinder and electric cord
    with glass slides

GEORGETTE
Handbag containing hat trimmed with ribbons and lace

<u>ACT II – Scene 5</u>

PRESET
Test tube emitting a bluish glow (on table)

COSTUME PLOT

ACT I – Scene 1 and Scene 2*

*PIERRE
Black worn-out overcoat with mittens tied to sleeves

GEORGETTE
Ordinary housekeeper's coat

BÉMONT
Winter coat

CHEVRIER
Impressive long coat

*MARIE
Black coat, black dress and black hat

ACT I – Scene 3

BÉMONT
A dapper outfit

ACT I – Scene 4

CHEVRIER
Ripped and tattered jacket, pants and top hat

BÉMONT
Smock that can easily be ripped to pieces

ACT I – Scene 5

MARIE
Same black coat

PIERRE
Same torn coat

ACT II – Scene 1 and Scene 2

MARIE
A nice summer dress

PIERRE
Shirt, sleeves rolled up

BÉMONT
Kid gloves, spats, grey pearl bowler hat

ACT II – Scene 3

PIERRE and MARIE
Clothing covered with dust

MARIE
A shawl covering her hair

ACT II – Scene 4

PIERRE and MARIE
Both cleaned up

ACT II – Scene 4

PIERRE and MARIE
Both wearing nice, clean coats

Set Drawing

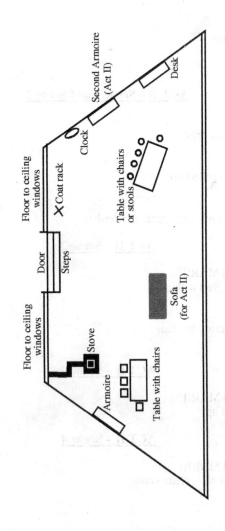